William Lockhart

Cardinal Newman

reminiscences of fifty years since

William Lockhart

Cardinal Newman
reminiscences of fifty years since

ISBN/EAN: 9783744741361

Printed in Europe, USA, Canada, Australia, Japan

Cover: Foto ©Raphael Reischuk / pixelio.de

More available books at **www.hansebooks.com**

CARDINAL NEWMAN:

REMINISCENCES OF FIFTY YEARS SINCE.

BY

ONE OF HIS OLDEST LIVING DISCIPLES,

WILLIAM LOCKHART, B.A., Oxon.

.

*To which is added, an Essay on a more recent
phase of the Oxford Movement.*

————

LONDON: BURNS & OATES, Limited.
NEW YORK: CATHOLIC PUBLICATION SOCIETY CO.

——

1891.

PREFACE.

On the death of the much beloved Cardinal, I was asked, as one of his oldest living disciples, to write an article on him in the *Paternoster Review*. No sooner was this sent to press, than I received a pressing request to write a Memoir for two other Periodicals. I tried to do my best ; of course some repetitions were unavoidable ; for these I hope my readers will make allowance.

I have reprinted the three Memoirs because some friends have thought that many would like to read them as a separate publication.

I have added an Essay on a more recent phase of the Oxford movement. The date will show that this last Essay was written before the Vatican Council.

W. L.

CARDINAL NEWMAN.*

A Retrospect of Fifty Years, by one of his oldest living disciples.

AFFECTIONATE veneration for my old Master in the Science of Truth, has made me wish to say something in honour of his memory; but I am now conscious that I have undertaken more than I can perform, except most imperfectly.

It is, I think, rather more than fifty years since I first had the privilege of knowing John Henry Newman. It was not long after I went to Oxford.

I saw him first on a certain day which I vividly remember. I was walking down High Street—it was between All Souls' and Queen's College. He was crossing, I think, to Oriel. My companion seized my arm, whispering to me, "Look, look there, that is Newman!" I looked, and there I saw him passing along in his characteristic way, walking fast, without any dignity of gait, but earnest, like one who had a purpose; yet so humble and self-forgetting in every portion of his external appearance, that you would not have thought him, at first sight, a man remarkable for anything.

It was only when you came to know him that you recognised or began to recognise what he was.

In speaking of my own reminiscences of Cardinal Newman and of his work, I shall necessarily have to speak of myself, but of myself

* Reprinted from the *Paternoster Review*, Oct., 1890.

merely as a type of the ordinary young Oxford man who came under Newman's wonderful influence.

For there was about him a spiritual power, an influence, or rather an effluence of soul, the force of moral greatness, which produced on some a feeling of awe in his presence. There was a tradition in my time at Oxford, that once on market day when the upper end of High Street, near Carfax Church, was much crowded with roughs, and the "Town" and "Gown" element were apt to come into collision, Newman was walking past All Saints' Church in the line of march of a furiously drunken butcher, who came up the street foul-mouthed and blasphemous. When they were near together, Newman stood in his path ; my informant, who was a "muscular Christian," the stroke of his college boat, expecting violence, came close up to the butcher, and was just making ready to fell him, when he saw the man stop short; Newman was speaking to him. Very quietly he said, "My friend, if you thought of the meaning of your words you would not say them." The savage was tamed on the spot; he touched his hat, turned round and went back.

When Whately was Principal of S. Alban Hall, Newman was his Vice-Principal. He was afterwards Tutor, and I think Dean, at Oriel; this brought him into contact with the undergraduates. Oriel especially was a "fashionable" college; there were always a good number of noblemen, baronets, gentlemen commoners, distinguished by their velvet, or "tufted" gold tasseled cap, and silk gown. They were mostly fast young men, "hunting in pink" was perhaps the smallest of their irregularities against university discipline. There was apt to be too much wine drunk at supper parties, and in consequence "rows in quad" were frequent. Newman could do more by a few words than any one living. "What did he say to you?" was asked of one who had been called up by Newman for some more or less serious matter. "I don't know," said the other, "but he looked at me."

Newman could read character; one felt in his presence that he read you through and through.

. In that wonderful passage in his "Discourses to Mixed Congregations," preached at Birmingham, he speaks out, with certain adaptations, what he had first learned of "polished ungodliness" in young Oxford men of rank, "tufts," as they were called, and of its bad imitations in the sometimes vulgar but superficially polished "tuft hunter," who was sent to Oxford, principally, that he might get "into good society and form useful connections." To the latter the following passage applies: "You my brethren have not been born splendidly; you have no high connections; you have not learned the manner or caught the tone of good society . . . . yet you ape the sins of Dives while you are strangers to his refinement . . . . you think it the sign of a gentleman to set yourself above religion . . . . to took at Catholic or Methodist with impartial contempt . . . . to walk up and down the street with your heads on high, and to stare at whatever meets you, and to say and do worse things, of which these outward extravagances are but the symbol!

"The Creator made you it seems, O my

children, for this office and work, to be a bad imitation of polished ungodliness."

And now one more word about Newman's personal appearance and his ways.

Who that has had experience of it can forget the impression made on him by the majesty of Newman's countenance, when one came really to know him and to study it—his meekness, his intensity, his humility, the purity of "a virgin heart in work and will" that was expressed in his eyes, his loving kindness, his winning smile, the wonderful sweetness and pathos, and delicate unstudied harmony of his voice!

Then he had, also, according to times and persons, a wonderful caressing way, which had in it nothing of softness, but which was felt to be a communication of strength from a strong soul, a thing that must be felt to be understood. Then there was at times in him a great vein of humour, and at times a certain playful way which he had of saying things which were full of meaning, and called to mind some passages in St. Paul's writings, suggesting, too, that perhaps there was in him, as in this, so also in other things, a certain likeness to the Great Apostle who made "himself all to all that he might gain all to God."

He impressed me in these ways more perhaps than any but one other man has impressed me —the great master of thought under whom I passed when I left Newman; another of the greatest minds of the age—Antonio Rosmini, the Founder of the Order to which I have the honour to belong.

When Newman read the Holy Scriptures from the lectern of St. Mary's or at Littlemore, we felt more than ever that his words were the words of a Seer, who saw God, and the things of God.

Many men are impressive readers, but we can see they *mean* to be impressive. They do not reach the soul; they play upon the sense and imagination: they are good actors, certainly; they may or may not be more. They do not forget themselves; you do not forget them.

Newman's reading of the Nicene Creed was a sublime meditation, or rather contemplation. I remember his reading the passage in the Book of Wisdom about the making of idols, and the sublime scorn with which he read of the " carving of the block of wood and the painting it with vermilion," impressed me with the blank stupidity of the attempt to put the idea of God, under any material form, and Newman's sermons were like his reading, the words of one who spoke with the utter conviction and intense earnestness —the quiet unstudied rhetoric—of one who saw truth and spoke what he saw.

These sermons were preached at St. Mary's, the University Church, at the afternoon parish service, when the University Sermon was over. It was always crowded by undergraduates, Bachelors and Masters of Arts, the very flower of "Young Oxford."

The effect of his teaching on us young men was to turn our souls, as it were, inside out; in measure and degree it was like what he says in the *Dream of Gerontius* of the soul after death presented before God,

> "Who draws the soul from out its case
> And burns away its stains."

God the Creator was the first theme he taught us, and it contained the premisses of all that followed. We never could be again the same as before, whether we "obeyed the heavenly vision" or neglected it.

We had gained some notion that there were false forms of Christianity to be avoided. Socinianism was one; Roman Catholicism was another; and this had been impressed upon us very strongly. But the Church of England, which we supposed was much the same in doctrine with the other Protestant Churches, we did not doubt was the old and true religion.

The next truth which we learned from the tenor of all his teaching was, that God who is so near us, that "in Him we live and move and are," who is the ultimate hidden force and First Cause beneath the phenomena of the visible universe, and of our own spiritual consciousness and conscience, our Moral Governor, might be expected beforehand to have given a religion to man by supernatural revelation.

He had done so. We accepted the Christianity of the Church of England as the original Revelation.

Being now convinced of the duties we owed to God and to Revelation, we set to work to practice the duties it taught—to repent of our sins and amend our lives, to pray very earnestly, and to frequent the Communion celebrated every Sunday morning early in the chancel of St. Mary's.

An important matter to us was the the teaching of Dr. Pusey on *Baptism* and on *Post-Baptismal Sin.* From hearing these doctrines, most of us came to hold that, as a fact, we had been made "temples of God in baptism."

What was our present condition, if by sin perhaps from early youth or even from childhood, we had driven out the Spirit of God and had become a dwelling place of evil spirits?

I do not know what to say about others; for myself no words can express the dark terror of my soul. But the Anglican doctrine, clear as it is about baptism, could tell us no remedy for sin committed after baptism.

It was for me most providential that I happened at this critical moment to come across a Roman Catholic book, Milner's *"End of Controversy."* I read it eagerly, for I was in sore distress. I saw at once, first, that I had been misled and mistaken as to the tenets of the Roman Catholics—that they believed in One God and in Jesus Christ as their only Redeemer and source of Grace; I saw that they taught that, in Baptism, we are made Temples of God, that sin deserves everlasting punishment, but that if we sin God has provided "a second plank after shipwreck," equivalent, if repentance is deep, to a second Baptism—the Holy Sacrament of Penance—Confession and Absolution.

This was the first time I had ever heard of this Sacrament. It was Milner who sent me to the Anglican Prayer-book for the same doctrine of Confession and Priestly Absolution, and then I saw it clearly laid down in the "Ordination Service of Priests" and in the "Office for the Visitation of the Sick." I afterwards read the same doctrine in the works of Jeremy Taylor, and of other Anglican Divines.

I was immensely relieved, and began to practise confession, but never without misgiving, since the first attempt I made with a very High

Church cathedral dignitary, who was so scared by my asking him to hear my confession that he said he really could not do it until he had consulted the Archdeacon! It was clear therefore that he had never met with anyone proposing to go to confession until that moment. What then was to be thought of a Church which had neglected for 300 years an essential Sacrament in which it professed in words to believe—what confidence could one have that in other weighty matters it had not neglected its trust?

This led me to see for the first time the meaning of the words in the Creed "I believe in One, Holy, Catholic, and Apostolic Church." I saw that the Roman Catholic Church was by far the largest portion of the Church of the Creed. I saw too that England was, up to the time of Henry VIII., a visible part of that Church. I supposed it was so still, or ought to be.

Doubts had begun to arise in my mind whether I ought not to become a Roman Catholic at once, for I could not see how the Church of England could still be a part of that Church from which it had separated. Still the example of Newman, and of so many, more learned and better far than myself, made me wish to be able honestly to dispel my doubts.

But that now happened in the Church of England which awoke us all from our dream that it formed any part of Catholic Christendom.

It was on this wise: The Established Church, by force of a new Act of Parliament, found itself committed by the consent of its Bishops to enter into communion with the German Lutherans and Calvinists, in the establishment of a Bishop of Jerusalem, consecrated by the Archbishop of

Canterbury, through a mandate of the Sovereign. This Bishop was to preside over a mixed community of Lutherans, Calvinists, and members of the Church of England, and to enter into communion, if they found the way open—if those heretics were willing—with Nestorians, Eutychians and other Oriental Christians.

In short, the act to which the State Church was absolutely committed, was, to faithful men in the Church of England, a revelation of the false step taken in the 16th Century, when the English Sovereign, with the full consent of the Bishops, made himself Head of the Church, through his law courts, "in all causes Ecclesiastical as well as Civil, supreme."

But Newman and others in good faith tried to content us, and prevent our leaving the Church of England; for he did not believe as yet that it was in schism, and though he was convinced that all Christendom ought to be united with the Bishop of Rome, he did not as yet see that out of that visible unity, the visible Church has no existence.

At this critical moment he published the famous "Tract 90," the object of which was to show that the Thirty-nine Articles of the Church of England were not irreconcilable with the Decrees of the Council of Trent, the last General Council of the Church; that the Articles were intended to include Roman Catholics if they would give up a certain technical dependence on the Bishop of Rome.

"Tract 90" produced an immense sensation throughout the country. This was quite unexpected by Newman. Edition on edition teemed from the press, and he was actually enabled with the proceeds to purchase a large and valuable library. It is that which was first at Littlemore, and is now at Edgbaston.

The heads of the University, however, and the Bishops now raised an universal protest against "Tract 90," and against all attempts to minimise the differences between the Church of England and the Catholic Church. Newman felt that his Eirenicon had failed.

On us young men "Tract 90" had the effect of strengthening greatly our growing convictions that Rome was right and the Church of England wrong.

Now, having taken my degree, I began for the first time very seriously to turn my mind to becoming a clergyman in the Church of England —or perhaps a Catholic priest. Hearing that Newman intended establishing a kind of monastery at Littlemore, near Oxford, I volunteered to join him, and was accepted.

We had now arrived at the year 1842, when we took up residence with Newman at Littlemore. Father Dalgairns and myself were the first inmates. It was a kind of monastic life of retirement, prayer and study. We had a sincere desire to remain in the Church of England, if we could be satisfied that in doing so we were members of the world-wide visible communion of Christianity which was of apostolic origin.

We spent our time at Littlemore in study, prayer and fasting. We rose at midnight to recite the Breviary Office, consoling ourselves with the thought that we were united in prayer with united Christendom, and were using the very words used by the Saints of all ages. We fasted according to the practice recommended in Holy Scripture, and practised in the most austere religious orders of Eastern and Western Christendom. We never broke our fast, except on Sundays and the Great Festivals, before twelve o'clock, and not until five o'clock in the Advent and Lenten seasons. We regularly practised confession, and went to Communion, I think, daily, at the Village Church. At dinner we met together, and after some spiritual reading at table, we enjoyed conversation with Newman. He spoke freely on all subjects that came up, but I think controversial topics were tacitly avoided. He was most scrupulous not to suggest doubts as to the position of the Church of England to those who had them not.

I remember him once saying that eternal punishment was to him of all Christian doctrines the most overwhelming; that not reason alone, but faith only, in God having revealed it by an infallible authority, could accept it.

Again, he once said that there were no doctrines of the Christian revelation which presented any thing like the intellectual difficulties that might be made to obscure the doctrine of God the Creator. Pantheism solved nothing; it only said, "We know nothing but what we see," and we can draw from it, only that what is, is." Newman would never let us treat him as a superior, but placed himself on a perfect level with the youngest of us. I remember that he insisted on our never calling him Mr. Newman, according to the custom of Oxford when addressing Fellows and Tutors of Colleges. He would have had us call him simply Newman. I do not think we ever ventured on this, though we dropped the Mr. and addressed him without any name.

It was his wish to give us some direct object of study (partly to keep us quiet) in his splendid library, in which were all the finest editions of the Greek and Latin Fathers, and School-men, all the best works on scripture and theology, general literature, prose and poetry, and a complete set of Bollandist "*Acta Sanctorum*," so far as they had been printed.

He had a project of bringing out *Lives of the English Saints*, and a translation of Fleury's *Ecclesiastical History*. I was set to work on the history of the Arian period, with a view to undertaking the translation of a volume.

Newman was an excellent violin player, and he would sometimes bring his violin into the library after dinner and entertain us with exquisite sonatas of Beethoven.

It is said that a well-known Protestant controversialist—Canon Hugh McNeill of Liverpool—a great spouter on anti-Popery platforms, once advised himself to challenge Newman to a public disputation. The great man's answer was like himself. He wrote saying that "Canon McNeill's well-known talent as a finished orator, would make such a public controversy an unfair trial of strength between them, because he himself was no orator. He had had in fact no practice in public speaking. His friends however told him that he was no mean performer on the violin, and if he agreed to meet Canon McNeill, he would only make one condition, that the Canon should open the meeting, and say all he had to say, after which he (Mr. Newman) would conclude with a tune on the violin.

The public would then be able to judge which was the best man."

I have said that Newman never alluded to Anglican difficulties, or unless pressed, in private, by direct questions. Once I had been to confession to him; and in other ways he knew I was in great distress about the position of the Church of England ever since I read Milner's "*End of Controversy.*" After I rose from my knees I said to him, "But are you sure that you can give me absolution?" He did not speak for a few moments, then he said in a tone of deep distress, "Why will you ask me, ask Pusey." This was the first indication I had received that he himself was seriously shaken as to his own position in the Anglican Church.

He soon perceived that I was more unsettled than ever. One day he came to my room and said, very kindly but abruptly, as if it was something unpleasant that he must say: "Now I must tell you that you must leave us at once, or else you must promise to remain with us for three years." I answered, "In my present state of mind I could not promise that." He said, "Will you go and see Ward and have a talk with him?" I assented, and the next day I went by appointment into Oxford to see Ward at Balliol. I remember he took me for a walk. I think we talked for three hours, walking round and round the Parks, beyond Wadham College. In the end, I found myself without an answer, thoroughly puzzled, but unconvinced. Ward had just published a huge volume, "*The Ideal Church,*" in which he made a great point of the relations between *Conscience* and *Intellect.* His line with me was, that I must know that however convinced in my intellect that I ought to leave the English Church, I must not trust it unless my conscience was up to the same measure as my intellect; and that, knowing myself, could I say that I had cultivated my conscience, by obedience to all that I knew was the Will of God, so as to justify me in being confident in the judgment of intellect?

I went back to Newman in a state of perplexed conscience; but not seeing what else to do, and hesitating in my judgment about the duty of submission to Rome, since I saw that such a learned, wise, and saintly man as Newman did not see it to be his duty, I gave him a promise to remain for the stipulated three years at Littlemore. Years after I found that Newman had not expected me to give the promise.

I kept my promise for about a year, but I was dreadfully unhappy. I thoroughly believed in sin and in Baptism, and that there was no revealed way for the washing away of post-baptismal sin except the Sacrament of Penance, Confession, and Absolution; now I doubted seriously about Anglican orders, but still more about Anglican jurisdiction, for I could see no Church on earth but the Visible Church, in which the successor of St. Peter is the Visible Head and Source of Jurisdiction, with the power of binding and of loosing given by Our Lord to His Visible Church under the Visible Head appointed by Him.

At last I could bear the strain no longer, and with great grief I left my dear Master, and was received into the Catholic Church in August, 1843.

Newman and my friends at Littlemore and

Oxford were greatly pained by my secession.
Newman considered himself so compromised by
it, that he immediately resigned his parish of
St. Mary's, and preached his last sermon—his
last sermon in the Anglican Church—at Littlemore. It is entitled "The Parting of Friends."

Two years later, in 1845, Newman and the rest
of his companions at Littlemore, and many
others, made their submission to the Catholic
Church. One of the first things he did after this
was to pay me a most kind and loving visit at
Ratcliffe College, near Leicester, where I was
studying.

He and many other learned disciples left the
Church of England, (and many others have
followed them,) because, through profound study,
and earnest seeking after God, during long
years of patient waiting, so as to test each step
thoroughly, they had come to be utterly convinced that the English Church had forfeited all
claim to teach, from the moment it separated
from the Visible Church, whose centre is at
Rome, its circumference the round world itself.
They saw that they had to leave the Church of
England as by Law Established under Henry
VIII. ; rather than join which Sir Thomas More,
Cardinal Fisher, and hundreds of others, priests
and laymen in England, Ireland, and Scotland
laid down their lives.

Our work among English Church people was
sundered. Few of the friends we had left cared
any longer to associate with us. We had become,
I will not say, "the scorn of men," for most men
believed we were sincere, however mistaken ;
but we were "the outcasts of our people." And
still more was this the case when the storm

arose throughout all England against the Catholics, on the occasion of the restoration of the English Hierarchy, and what was called the *Papal Aggression* Act of Parliament. But a reaction came: the New Act against Catholics was ignominiously expunged from the Statute Book, as the result of this revulsion of public opinion. After a time, too, we found our old friends, long estranged, venturing to come near us again.

But no event, and no person, has had so much to do with producing this revulsion of public feeling as Cardinal Newman. Nothing is needed to prove this beyond the daily papers and reviews of this month, which show that his death has been treated by the public opinion of England as the loss of one of the greatest, most venerated of England's sons. Yet he was a Catholic, a convert, a Cardinal of Rome, and the writer who has done more to expose the errors of Protestantism than any writer for three centuries.

But during the greater part of the past fifty years the work even of Newman, and still more of the most of us, as priests in the Catholic Church, has been chiefly among the masses of the Irish Catholics resident in England, and the faithful remnant of the old English Catholics.

Yet, as we have ministered to Catholic congregations, many of all classes, and of all Protestant denominations, and many from the ranks of Socinians, and of Rationalists of every degree, have come to us, by all manner of different roads, and lines of thought, and, convinced by the same ultimate reasons that convinced us, have become Catholics.

. But in the Church of England itself, the work

of Newman is not over. He has done much
to save it from the deteriorating spirit of a
State religion, tending fast to Socinianism and
Rationalism, and raised in it a desire widely
felt to prove itself a part of the Catholic Church.
English Churchmen, generally, have a pervad-
ing consciousness that they are in the presence
of the majestic Visible Unity of the Catholic
Church. That was not the case fifty years ago.

Meantime great numbers of the ministers of
the Church of England, with the prestige of
their position, teach publicly nearly every one
of those Catholic doctrines which our forefathers
abandoned 300 years ago. They delight to call
themselves Catholics, and to think that they are
one in doctrine with the ancient Church, from
the days of St. Augustine up to the days of
Henry VIII. Perhaps there is but one doctrine
they have not yet reached—the key-stone of the
arch—the See of Peter—the centre and the test
of Catholic Unity.

Let us hope that in the Church of England,
men are as earnest, now, in seeking after dogmatic truth, and " the Church of the Living God
the pillar and ground of the truth," as those
who were the first leaders in the *Catholicizing*
Movement of fifty years since.

Well, it took Newman and Manning many
years to reach this point, after they had, already,
come to believe most Catholic doctrines.

Yet, men of thought and earnestness cannot
put themselves into our position of fifty years
ago. The case of the *Jerusalem Bishopric*, and
the *Gorham case*, were a *revelation* that the
Church of England has its public teaching
authority solely from the State. Its clergy

may teach almost every Catholic doctrine, because all doctrines have been reduced to such opinions on *religion* as public opinion, and the House of Commons, which roughly, but clearly enough represents public opinion, will tolerate; and it will tolerate nearly everything, short of open atheism and downright Popery.

CARDINAL NEWMAN :*

A Reminiscence of Oxford of Fifty Years Ago.

I AM glad to be allowed to say a word in loving veneration of one to whom under God I owe my soul. Through having been providentially brought under his influence at Oxford, fifty years ago, I was guided to escape the quicksands of Rationalism, and to find the secure haven of the Catholic Church.

I went to Oxford in 1838, when Newman's influence was at its highest point. His great name drew me to his sermons, which he preached every Sunday evening at the parish service of St. Mary's, after the University Sermon was over. Newman's sermons were attended by great numbers of under-graduates, bachelors and masters of arts, the flower of young Oxford. They were wonderful, not because of any studied rhetoric or arts of eloquence, but because of their quiet earnestness. They spoke of God, as no man, I think, could speak, unless God were with him ; unless he were a Seer, like the prophets of old, and saw God.

For aboriginal Catholics, it is not easy to understand many of the characteristics of the life and influence of John Henry Newman ; especially the long course of years it took him, and many others who are now Catholics, to find their way through the tangled mazes of religious

* Reprinted from the *Irish Ecclesiastical Record*, October, 1890.

error in which they had been brought up, and reach, at last, the City of God, which to Catholics seems so manifestly "the City set upon a hill which cannot be hid." The Catholic who has received the Faith in his baptism, and has adhered from the earliest opening of his reason to the *motivum credendi*, *i.e.*, God speaking to him by the Light of Faith within his soul, and by His infallible Church, cannot easily place himself in the position of a convert, who has climbed up to the high mountain, whence by the intuition of faith he sees God and the things of God, and holds them no longer as *opinions*, but as *verities*. To the Catholic, all seems so clear, because he has seen all from the first glowing in the Light of Faith.

If ever he examines the *motiva credibilitatis*, or formal evidences of religion, wishing to have a well-ordered, reflected view of the reasons why he believes, it is never tentatively, *i.e.*, taking the things of faith hypothetically; this would be for him an act against faith. But the convert has had to take all the articles of faith, in the first instance, hypothetically; he has had to weigh their probabilities *pro* and *contra*, and it was only through finding a multitude of probabilities all converging in one point, that he felt at last compelled by the exigence of duty towards truth and the God of truth, to give assent to the truth of revelation as a whole and in its parts—and to make his Act of Faith in the Catholic Church. But it may, perhaps, seem curious to Catholics, and a thing unexpected, that converts generally come to the Church, through being satisfied on *details*. They, *e.g.*, find, first of all—perhaps by reading some

Catholic exposition or catechism—that the Church does *not* teach the errors they had supposed, that it is not idolatrous or anti-Christian; that, on the contrary, it holds all the doctrines of Christianity that Protestants themselves hold as essential. So that if ever they became Catholics, they would have to give up nothing that they had always believed, but would only have to add to their faith some matters, which Catholics assert to be necessary logical consequences of the other doctrines which are not in dispute—and which are taught in the writings of the early centuries of Christianity—such, as these are, *e.g.*, the doctrines of the Real Presence, the Sacrifice of the Mass, Prayers for the Dead, Purgatory, Invocation of the Saints, and the Infallibility of the Church and of its Head.

When the mind of one who seeks truth has come to this point, he has also become convinced that the Church which has its centre at Rome forms by far the largest portion of Christendom, and the burden of proof is shifted; he is bound to defend his position, to show good reason for his protest and for his remaining outside the great communion of united Christendom. Such, more or less, has been the course by which we have had to pass. The Oxford movement was most important, because it was the first large and important *exodus* of Protestants, and of their return to the communion of the Mother Church. Newman was leader of a band of pioneers who cut their way, with great expenditure of time and labour, through the tangled forest that had grown up during three hundred years, between the insular Christianity of England and Catholic Christendom.

Another point, which comes to some Catholics as a surprise, is, when, in persons who are outside the visible Church, and involved in many erroneous opinions on religion, they find the most evident marks of Christian sanctity. John Henry Newman was an instance of this. No one who knew him could doubt that he was one in whom "wisdom had built herself a house;" as the Incarnate Wisdom says of the man who loves God: "My Father will love him, and We will come to him, and make Our abode with him." Of course, "out of the Church there is no salvation," and "without faith, it is impossible to please God;" but it is also true that those who are in invincible ignorance of the truth, considered as a whole, may yet hold what they do hold, by divine faith, through the grace of their baptism. These are no heretics, if they have never knowingly and wilfully rejected the truth. They are in a salvable condition, are implicit Catholics, *i.e.*, Catholics as God knows them. They belong to "the soul of the Church," as St. Augustine says, though they form no visible part of the Church's visible body.

Again, it must be remembered that men in Newman's position, who come into the Catholic Church chiefly through the elaborate study of the Fathers and of ecclesiastical history, find many difficulties that have to be reconciled, knotty points of history that have to be disentangled; especially, since many of the most telling arguments of Protestants against the Church are drawn from an elaborate, if one-sided, study of Ecclesiastical History, of documents of Fathers and of Popes.

Then, among historical difficulties, are to be

noted the many scandals in the lives of Bishops and Popes, at particular periods; and all these are far greater difficulties to those without the Church, than they are to us who are within, and not looking out for the Church, but who know it, and possess it. *We* remember, always, the words of our Lord, that the kingdom of heaven on earth, was to be like to "a net cast into the sea, gathering into it good fish and bad;" and again, it was to be like "cockle, growing in the midst of the good seed, until the harvest." A real survey of the almost boundless field of history is a gigantic work; and it is this which detained Newman so long upon the road. But it is not the road for ordinary wayfarers. It had to be done once for all, and John Henry Newman has done it, and has made a high-road for all time, by which men of good-will can easily find their way, even through the mazes of history, from the City of Confusion to the City of Truth.

I have a vivid remembrance of my first seeing John Henry Newman when I was quite a youth at Oxford. He was pointed out to me in the High-street. I should not have noticed him if his name had not been mentioned by my companion. He was walking fast, with a very peculiar gait, which was his own. It was like a man·walking fast in slippers, and not lifting his heel. It was not dignified; but you saw at a glance that he was a man intent on some thought, and earnest in pursuing some purpose, but who never gave a thought as to what impression he was making, or what people thought about him. When one came to know and study him, it was plain that his mind was so *objective* that his own subjectivity was well-nigh forgotten.

Hence his simplicity, meekness, and humility;
God, not self, was the centre of all his thoughts.

Newman's sermons had the most wonderful
effect on us young men. It was to many of us
as if God had spoken to us for the first time. I
could never have believed beforehand, that it
was possible that a few words, read very quietly
from a manuscript, without any rhetorical effort,
could have so penetrated our souls. I do not
see how this could have been, unless he who
spoke was himself a *seer*, who saw God, and the
things of God, and spoke that which he had seen,
in the keen, bright, intuition of faith. We felt
God speaking to us; turning our souls, as it
were, "inside out," cutting clean through the
traditions of human society, which are able so
completely to corrupt and distort the spiritual
insight of the soul.

The great defect of Protestant training is, that
no one (I speak of fifty years since) ever spoke
clearly of the essential immorality of all impurity. Certain things which injured life, health, or
reputation, were reprobated; nothing else was
ever hinted at. There was, of course, no training
of the Confessional, by which, chiefly, with
Catholics, this evil is very often nipped in the
bud. For the Catholic child knows by the instinct of faith, and through the few modest
words said to him by teachers or parents when
he is preparing to make his examination of conscience before confession, that *immodest thoughts*
even, if deliberately indulged in, would be mortal
sin. This is the great defence of Catholic
morality; it is "a fortification with a strong
outwork"—*murus et ante-murale*. The absence
of this training left English Protestant society

in a very corrupted state. It was, indeed, considered *bad form*, among gentlemen, to talk of
impurity; the grossness of language and the
drunken orgies of a previous generation had
passed away. But there was a kind of tacit
understanding among middle-aged men, fathers
of families, clergymen, &c., that it would not do
to be too hard on the young ; that we must keep
our blind eye on the doings of our young sons,
that "youths must sow their wild oats." They
would learn prudence and wisdom by experience,
as their elders had done, and they would turn
out as well as these old squires, and "grave and
reverend seniors," felt, complacently, they had
done. While I say this, let me bear testimony
to the extraordinary purity, in those days, among
the women of the upper and middle classes ; the
classes from which the clergy of the Church of
England of that time chiefly came. Especially,
I remember, that the daughters of the families of
the clergy, and of the country gentry, were models
of English gentlewomen, brought up under home
influences; while the sons, educated at public
schools, were far below their sisters in education,
refinement, and Christian morals and piety.
The public, and still more the private schools
were such, that it was rare, indeed, if any innocent youth passed through them without being
stained ; too often he was utterly corrupted.

It was of such materials that the youth of
Oxford were chiefly composed ; and on such as
these Newman's sermons came down like a new
revelation. He had the wondrous, the supernatural power of raising the mind to God, and of
rooting deeply in us a personal conviction of God,
and a sense of His Presence. He compelled us

to an intuitive perception of moral obligation—of that Natural Law of right, which is written in the mind by the Word and Wisdom of God, and which St. Augustine and St. Thomas say is the "Reason of the Divine Wisdom, imparted to man by the light of Human Reason dictating what is right and what is wrong."

It was not at first sight that Newman's personal appearance struck me. It was only when I came to hear him and study his countenance that I understood its majesty, and saw in him a something different from any human being I had ever known. Everything about him was unstudied, self-forgetting. To see him come into St. Mary's, in his long white surplice, was like nothing one had seen before. He seemed to glide in swiftly like a spirit incarnate; for with him it was the spirit that had the power of impressing you. When he reached the lectern, in the middle aisle, he would drop down on his knees, and remain fixed in mental prayer for a few moments; then he rose in the same strange unearthly way, and began the evening service. His reading of the lessons from the Old and New Testament, as I have heard him many a time at Oxford and at Littlemore, was the most marvellous expression of soul. It showed how imperfect a medium of ideas are words in themselves; it is only soul can speak to soul; and some men, but very few like Newman in this, have the power of using words, as some extraordinary violinists are said to have used their instruments, so as to draw forth sounds that would have seemed beyond the reach of earthly music.

Newman had the power of so impressing your soul as to efface himself, and you thought only of that majestic soul that saw God. You felt that it was God speaking to you, as He speaks in all the wonderful handwriting of the book of nature, but in a deeper way, by the articulate voice of man made to the *image*, raised to the *likeness* of God; conveying, through intelligence, and sense, and imagination, and the voice of words, which are the most efficacious signs of ideas, a *transcript*, as it were, of the architypal thoughts of God.

Never shall I forget hearing him read the first chapter of the Book of Genesis: "In the beginning God created... and the Spirit of God moved over the face of the waters:" and that wonderful chapter in the Epistle to the Hebrews, "God, who at sundry times and in diverse manners spake in times past to our fathers by the prophets, hath in these last days spoken unto us by His Son... But to the Son He saith, Thy throne, O God, is for ever and ever." The faith in the One God, and in the One Lord Jesus Christ, God of God, came home to many of us, in his reading, as it had never before come home when we had heard the Creed read, or repeated these dogmas of the faith in our catechism.

What struck me as the characteristic of his whole teaching and influence was, that he made us think, reflect, know that we knew, or that we did not know; thus he led us to seek for the *last reasons of things*, and so on to the Last Reason of all things—the First Cause of all—God the Creator. This was the first thing he did for us young men; he rooted in us a personal faith and knowledge of God, a sense of His presence, and of the exigency of our duty to Him, in all things, in and for Him. As we had thus learned practically to know God, we felt the urgent need of further knowledge of God than nature could give us. We accepted Christianity as being, in fact, beyond the shadow of doubt, God's last revelation of Himself to man. If God was present in man, by the light of nature and of grace, and if the voice of conscience is the voice of God, what more probable than that He should have sent His final message to man, by a Man, who was Personally "God manifest in the flesh?" Christianity, we doubted not; and the Christianity of the Church of England we doubted not, was that which was taught by Christ and His Apostles. We had some notion that all Protestant sects were substantially one in doctrine, differing chiefly on matters of Church government. We believed, however, that there were certain corrupted forms of Christianity that had to be avoided as a pestilence; especially that of Roman Catholics, who had lapsed into idolatry, worshipped the Virgin Mary in place of God, and belonged to an apostate church, the anti-Christian apostacy foretold in prophecy. We, therefore, set to work to try our best to be good Church of England Christians, to repent of our sins and to amend our lives, to pray earnestly, and to frequent the Communion as it was celebrated every Sunday by Newman in the chancel of St. Mary's.

Just at this time a series of sermons preached and published by Dr. Pusey on *Baptismal Regeneration*, and *Post-Baptismal Sin* were making a great impression. We were convinced that these doctrines were clearly those of the Church of England, of the Scripture, and of the early Fathers of the Christian Church. It was clear that by baptism we had been made temples of God, as St. Paul also teaches. But then had we not banished God's Spirit, and made our soul a temple of devils?

The Church of England had nothing to tell us, as to how post-baptismal sin was to be remitted. Providentially for me, a Roman Catholic book had come into my hands—*Milner's End of Controversy*. I had taken it away from a great friend of mine, who had received it from a Catholic priest in London. My friend became a Catholic shortly after. He is Ignatius Grant, S.J. In this book I read a full exposition of what Catholics believe. I found that I had been completely misled, and that they really held all Christian doctrines which Protestants consider essential. I also saw clearly that there had always been in the Christian Church the belief and the practice of the sacrament of penance, confession, and absolution, by which the sins committed after baptism could be remitted. Milner also shewed me that in the Church of England Prayer-Book, the whole doctrine of the power of absolution conferred by Christ on the priesthood was plainly laid down in the *Ordination Service;* and the practice of auricular confession, in order to obtain absolution, was set forth in the *Office for the Visitation of the Sick.* The reading of this book effected a revolution in my mind. It was difficult to believe in a Church which, while laying down the doctrine of absolution and of confession as necessary for all who needed it by reason of grievous sin, had so utterly neglected it in practice, that I, educated among religious people, had never heard of it until I read about it in a Catholic book. I saw, moreover, that if the Roman Catholic Church was not an apostate Church, it was by far the largest portion of the Church, and I could not see how the Church of England could be justified in separating from the Pope, and from the greater part of the Church, at the bidding of the Tudor sovereigns.

During all this time we had all been following the line taken by the *Tracts for the Times*. The main argument of these publications was, that the Church of England, in the Creeds, and in her Articles, Canons, and Homelies, professes to follow the doctrines taught by the Fathers of the first four or five centuries. We had read enough of these authorities to see that they clearly taught nearly every doctrine held by the Roman Catholic Church ; and it seemed to us evident that the Bishop of Rome had always held a primacy of jurisdiction or supremacy over the whole Church. Many of us were, therefore, disposed to become Catholics at once.

Newman had not as yet come to see that separation from Rome involved separation from the visible Church, and as long as he did not see this, he thought himself bound to remain where he was, and to use his influence to retain others in the Church of England. It was with this view that he published the famous *Tract* 90, the object of which was to show that the Thirty-nine Articles of the Church of England were not irreconcilable with the degrees of the Council of Trent ; that the Articles were intended to include Roman Catholics, if they were willing to give up the Roman obedience, which he thought concerned rather the temporal accidents of spiritual things.

Tract 90 produced an immense sensation throughout the country. But after a time the

THE QUADRANGLE OF ORIEL COLLEGE, OXFORD.

heads of the University and the bishops raised a universal protest against it, and against all attempts to minimize the differences between the Church of England and the Catholic Church. Newman felt that his *Eirenicon* had failed.

On us young men *Tract* 90 had the effect of strengthening greatly our growing convictions that Rome was right, and the Church of England wrong. But we were immensely influenced by our respect for Newman's learning and conscientiousness, and were willing to try all we could to be contented in the Church of England, if it were possible to show that it was a portion of the visible Church. Several of us, with this view, put ourselves under Newman, at Littlemore, near Oxford. This was a kind of monastic life of prayer, fasting, and study. We rose at midnight to say the Divine Office. We fasted always till 12 o'clock, except on Sundays and great festivals; till 5 o'clock during Advent and Lent. The rest of the time we passed in study.

I soon found that Newman himself was seriously shaken as to the position of the Church of England. This confirmed all my previous doubts and convictions, and made me feel that it was my duty to make my act of submission to the Church, Catholic and Roman. Two years later, Newman and his companions at Littlemore were received into the Church.

CARDINAL NEWMAN; OR, "'TIS FIFTY YEARS SINCE."*

AMONG the many indications marking the different phases of religious thought in England, perhaps none is more noteworthy than the way in which the death of our venerable Cardinal has been received by the English non-Catholic public. The public press, the surest test of public opinion, when all political and religious parties are agreed on any point, has spoken unmistakably its estimate of this great Catholic, and of the work of his lifetime. They have spoken of his death as a public loss, the passing away of one of the grandest intellects of our age, worthy to be ranked with an Origen, an Athanasius, an Augustine—of a soul most lovable and tender, straightforward, honest and truthful to conscience in all that he has done or written.

But the words of our beloved Cardinal Archbishop, spoken in the London Oratory, at the Solemn Mass of Requiem, say all this better far than words of mine.

"If any proof were needed of the immeasurable work that John Henry Newman has wrought in England, the last week would be enough. None could doubt that the great multitude of his personal friends in the first half of his life, and the still greater multitude of those who have been instructed, consoled, and won to God by

* Reprinted from the *Dublin Review*, Oct., 1890.

the unequalled beauty, the irresistible persuasion of his writings, at such a time as this, would pour out the love and gratitude of their hearts.

"But that the public voice of England, political and religious, in all its diversities, should, for once, unite in love and veneration of a man who had broken through its sacred barriers and defied its religious prejudices, who could have believed it?

"He had committed the unpardonable sin in England. He had rejected the whole Tudor Settlement in religion. He had become Catholic, as our fathers were; and yet, for no one in our memory has such a heartfelt and loving veneration been poured out. Some one (a non-Catholic writer) has said: 'Whether Rome canonises him or not, he will be canonised in the thoughts of pious people of many creeds in England.' This is true; but I will not therefore say that the mind of England is changed. Nevertheless, it must be said that, towards a man who has done so much to estrange it, the will of the English people was changed; the old malevolence had passed into good will.

"If this is a noble testimony to a great Christian life, it is as noble a proof of the justice, equity, and uprightness of the English people. In venerating John Henry Newman it has unconsciously revealed and honoured itself.

"In the history of this great life, and of all that it has done, we cannot forget that we owe to him, among other debts, one singular achievement. No one who does not intend to be laughed at, will henceforward say that the Catholic religion is fit only for weak intellects and unmanly brains. This superstition of pride is

D

over   The author of the 'Grammar of Assent'
may make them think twice before they so
expose themselves. Again, the designer and
editor of the 'Library of the Fathers' has planted
himself on the undivided Church of the first six
centuries; and he holds the field; the key of the
position is lost."

These are great words, pregnant of meaning.
They will be remembered in connection with our
two great Cardinals, so long as the "History of
England" is read. For they mark the last half
century of England's history and of the history
of religion, which is inseparable from that of the
English people, in whom is so deeply rooted the
natural religious instinct.

Every thinking man in England is either a
believer or a non-believer in Christianity. Few
profess to be indifferent on the matter. Few are
disbelievers in Christianity; fewer still are
Atheists. Every man, even if he is a non-believer,
yet a man of some education and reflection,
knows that Christianity has been the religion of
all the most enlightened nations of the world for
the greater part of twenty centuries, and of most
of their greatest men, philosophers, statesmen,
men of learning, and letters.

. He knows that it began with the poor; at the
first, "not many rich, not many noble, not many
learned were called." But gradually it spread
among the learned and the noble, who were
converted through beholding the lives of extraordinary virtue and heroism even to martyrdom,
of poor working men and women, the modesty
of Christian virgins, many of them, both men
and women, their own slaves, as most of the
working-class were in those ages of Imperial

Rome. He knows that it was nothing but Christianity that created Christendom, where Heathendom had lain, infecting for ages all God's fair earth, like the corrupting bones and corpses in Ezekiel's vision.

It was Christianity that bid these corpses rise and live, that breathed into the dead world the Spirit from God, the spirit of charity and of liberty. For liberty is man's conscious power of self-government, through aid of a new light and a new force, which was not in human nature before the coming of Christ. It was this new consciousness of the "perfect law of liberty," of "the liberty of the children of God," which gave to every Christian an intimate sense of right, and of duty to God and to all that God had made, and to "the powers that be, which are ordained by God." It taught the right of every man to live and to possess the fruits of his toil; and in matters between his soul and God, to follow his own conscience, to be free from all human dictation in matter of religion. Such was the Charter of the Gospel, and such was the Christianity which was the creation of the Gospel, and which converted the world.

But there are some who admit all this, as historical fact, and yet say, we do not believe any longer in Christianity. If they are asked why, they will say, because Christianity, now, is not like Primitive Christianity. We could believe in that as a revelation from heaven. It proved itself by its fruits. It appealed to the people, to the working classes, to the masses of mankind. It was the very mark of Christ's religion that "to the poor the Gospel was preached," It endured three hundred years of martyrdom, yet it conquered the world; its strength was in weakness; it could not be human, it could not but have been divine.

So reasoned the men of the Oxford movement, when they began to put out the *Tracts for the Times* in 1833, and it was the spirit of John Henry Newman that inspired that whole movement.

These men of the Church of England believed firmly in Christianity as a divine revelation, and in Christ, as " God manifest in the Flesh "— " Emmanuel, God with us." They studied the New Testament, and the Primitive Christian writers, who were the immediate disciples of the Apostles and of their immediate successors; the writings of St. Ignatius, the disciple of St. John, of St. Irenæus his disciple, and St. Justin, the martyr. They went on to study SS. Cyprian, Cyril, Athanasius, Augustine, and the rest.

It was to this study that they were sent by the authoritative canons of the Church of England, as the best commentaries on Scripture, and the rule that the founders of the Anglican Church professed to have followed.

The men of the Oxford movement had thus formed for themselves in their own minds what they believed to be the typical form of Primitive Christianity.

They turned then to compare it with the Christianity of the Church of England, and the more they contemplated the contrast, the more were they astounded and horrified at the prospect before them. They asked why was this. They did not stop at details, but went at once to the last reason of the thing.

They observed that the supreme characteristic

of Primitive Christianity was an intense conviction that the Church was a divine power in the world : the visible kingdom of the God of heaven foretold by Daniel, gifted by its Divine Author with "the Spirit of truth," of which Christ had said: "I will send to you the Spirit of truth, that He may guide you into all truth, and that He may abide with you for ever;" and again, in our Lord's last words ever spoken on earth, "All power is given to Me in heaven and upon earth; go ye therefore and teach all nations, baptising them in the name of the Father and of the Son and of the Holy Ghost, teaching them to observe all things I have commanded you, and, behold, I am with you all days, even to the end of the world."

They turned to St. Irenæus, the disciple of St. Polycarp, who was himself the disciple of St. John, and who wrote within fifty years of the Apostles. They found there, set forth, in the most luminous manner, that Primitive Christianity adhered to the teaching of a living body, already called the Catholic or universal Church, spread everywhere. Pagan writers like Tacitus, Suetonius, and Pliny have testified to this, as a fact known to all, within fifty years of the death of Christ. Of the Church Irenæus speaks as a witness, from within, to the same fact to which Pagan historians witnessed, from without. "This preaching and this faith, once delivered to the Apostles by Christ, the Church having received, though she be spread throughout the whole world, carefully guards, as inhabiting *one* house, as having *one* soul, and the *same* heart, and delivers down as having *one* mouth. Nor have the Churches of Germany believed otherwise, nor of Spain, nor Gaul, nor in the East, nor in Egypt, nor in Syria, nor those of the middle of the world. But, as the sun, God's creature, throughout the world, is one and the same: so, too, the preaching of the truth shines everywhere and enlightens all men that are willing to come to the knowledge of the truth."

"There being such proofs to look to, we ought not to seek elsewhere for the truth, which it is easy to receive from the Church, since the Apostles most fully committed unto this Church, as unto a rich storehouse, all which is of the truth. For this is the gate of life; all the rest are thieves and robbers. They must, therefore, be avoided; but whatever may be of the Church, we must love with the utmost diligence, and lay hold of the tradition of the truth."

The teaching of St. Irenæus was seen to be one and the same with that of the earlier and later Fathers. I have selected his words, because they witness to the belief of the whole Church of the second century, of the Eastern portion of Christendom, of which Irenæus was a native, and of the Western portion also, for he was Bishop of Lyons in Gaul, where he wrote, and where he suffered martyrdom.

The men of the Oxford movement saw that Christians were no longer a united body, that the Protestant principle of the Bible, interpreted by each man's private judgment, had utterly destroyed all unity of doctrine, and all idea of any divine authority residing in the Church and having the power and right to say what interpretations of Scripture were right, and what were wrong. Hence the endless multitude of Dissenting Sects in England, all offshoots from the Established Church.

They saw, too, that in the Church of England, the whole power of deciding what was to be taught in that Church, was vested in the Sovereign, by Act of Parliament, and depended in reality on the varying phases of public opinion, as represented by Parliament.

It seemed to them that the only thing to be done was to appeal to the Christian public opinion of the country, and to endeavour powerfully to act upon that. This decided them to put forward, in the "Tracts for the Times," in the clearest manner, the contrast between Primitive Christianity and the actual Christianity of the Church of England.

It was for the same reason that Newman projected and carried out the great work of translating the principal Fathers of the early centuries.

When Newman projected the "Library of the Fathers" he had certainly not the smallest suspicion that the movement would issue, through logical sequence, from premiss to conclusion, in his obligation in conscience to become, what he would then have called, a Roman Catholic.

This comes out clearly in his "Apologia," and in his "Anglican Difficulties," and it is noteworthy, because Newman has often been accused of being a Papist in disguise. He tells us that, when he began the "Tracts for the Times," in 1833, he believed that the Church of the Roman Communion was anti-Christian and idolatrous, in fact, that the Pope was the Anti-Christ of prophecy.

In the December of the year before, he had started with his friend Hurrell Froude, and others, on a tour in Italy, and spent some time in Rome. He received no religious impressions there. He says: "We kept out of the way of Catholics throughout our tour." He went, in short, as most tourists go, with all the prejudices in which he had been brought up, and which he never doubted were a true and just view of things. He saw all things through this medium of prejudice, and came back as he had started. He says, speaking of his stay in Rome: "As to Church services, we attended the *Tenebræ* at the Sistine Chapel, but for the sake of the *Miserere*, that was all." He went only to hear the famous music of the Papal choir, which, as a born musician, he was able fully to appreciate. He says: "My general feeling was 'All, save the spirit of man, is divine.'" He parted from his friends in Rome, and made a journey by himself through Sicily. There, he was taken dangerously ill with fever. His servant thought he would die, but he kept saying to himself: "I shall not die; I have a work to do in England. I shall not die, for I have not sinned against light." In his illness in Sicily he was visited by the priest of the place, who had heard, probably from his Catholic servant, that an Englishman was dying, and would not send for a priest. Newman was too ill to talk. He says: "I felt inclined to enter into controversy with him." But he had no thought of availing himself of his spiritual services. Referring to his Diary (June, 1833) he says: "I was aching to get home. I felt I had a work to do. At Palermo I was kept three weeks waiting for a vessel. I began to visit the churches, and they calmed my impatience. I did not attend any service. I knew nothing of the Blessed Sacrament there.

At last I got off in an orange-boat bound for Marseilles. We were becalmed in the Straits of Bonifacio. Then it was that I wrote the lines, 'Lead, kindly light, amid the encircling gloom.'"

He arrived, at last, at Oxford, about the second week of July. He writes: "On the following Sunday (July 14), Mr. Keble preached the 'Assize Sermon' in the University pulpit. It was published under the title of 'National Apostacy.' I have ever considered and kept that day as the start of the religious movement of 1833."

It was now that the work began, on which he had been ruminating during his journey and his illness, when he said: "I have a work to do in England. I shall not die; I have not sinned against the light."

> Lead, kindly light, amid the encircling gloom
> Lead thou me on.
> I do not ask to see the distant scene,
> *One step* enough for me.

"One step" was clear to him. It was to act, as we have said above, on Christian public opinion, and, if possible, bring back England to the truth, unity, and fervour of Primitive Christianity. The means he devised for this end was principally the "Tracts for the Times," and the "Translations of the Early Fathers." Another most important instrument was placed in his hands—the parochial pulpit of St. Mary's University and parish church, of which he had been appointed Vicar. Newman's beautiful series of historical sketches called the "Church of the Fathers" was published for the same end. He says: "The 'Church of the Fathers' is one of the earliest productions of the movement, and appeared, in numbers, in the *British Magazine*, being written with the aim of introducing the religious sentiments, views, and customs of the first ages of the Church into the modern Church of England."

The translation of Fleury's "Church History" was also projected, and intended to make English Churchmen familiar with the history of the early councils of the Church, of the controversies on which they pronounced definite judgment, and by which the creeds used in the Anglican Church were framed and developed, in order more fully to define the "faith once delivered" by the Apostles, and thus to meet each new attack of rationalising heresy. Thus the work progressed from 1833 to 1841. Of this time, Newman writes : "So I went on for years up to 1841. It was, in a human point of view, the happiest time of my life. . . . . We prospered and spread. . . . . The Anglo-Catholic party (as it is called) suddenly became a power in the National Church, and an object of alarm to her rulers and friends. . . . It seemed as if those doctrines were in the air, and that the movement was the birth of a crisis rather than of a place or party. In a very few years, a school of opinion had been formed, fixed in its principles, indefinitive and progressive in their range ; and it extended itself into every part of the country. Nay, the movement and its party-names (Puseyite, Newmanite, Tractarian), were known to the police of Italy, and to the backwoodmen of America. . . . . And so it proceeded, getting stronger and stronger every year, till it came into collision with the nation and the Church of the nation; which it began by professing, especially, to serve."

The "Tracts for the Times" and the "Library of the Fathers" obtained a wide circulation, and formed a school in the Church of England. They may be said to have, in a sense, created the present Church of England. For very few Churchmen would now deny that Christianity is essentially connected with a visible Church, which, at least in General Council, would be infallible. The claim of every Churchman is, that the Church of England is a part of the Catholic Church of the days of SS. Irenæus, Cyprian, and Cyril, and the rest.

They avoid thinking of their separation from the rest of Christendom, under the ".Tudor settlement" of the Church of England, "by law established" and by authority of Parliament, as a National Church. They have no theory of the Visible Unity of the Church, which fits in with the visible fact of disunion, and they take refuge in words which, if they mean anything, have reference only to the invisible Church, which Catholics also admit, but in which they would charitably include every soul that is right with God, dissenters of all shades, and possibly even some Pagans, according to the teaching of the great Jesuit theologians, such as De Lugo, Suarez, and others.

But to return to our narrative. Several important public events brought out more and more clearly, in the minds of Newman and of those who acted with him, the absolute *Erastianism*, or complete dependence on the State, of the Church of England. The Whigs were in office; Liberalism in religion was in the ascendant. The appointment of Dr. Hampden, one of the leading clergy of the Liberal or Broad Church school, suspected of Arian or Socinian leanings, to a bishopric, against the vehement protest of the University of Oxford and of many of the bishops, showed this complete servitude to the State, and to the Prime Minister of the day, who happened to have a majority in the House of Commons.

Then came a project of the Government, to which the bishops assented, to establish, in concert with Prussia, an Anglican bishop at Jerusalem, who was to rule over Lutherans, Calvinists, and Anglicans, and to hold communion, if they saw their way, with Nestorians, and Eutychians—heretics condemned by the General Councils, by which the Anglican Church, in her canons, professed to be bound. An Act of Parliament was passed to enable the Archbishop of Canterbury, by royal authority, to consecrate this bishop. The Archbishop consented, saying, as he had said in the case of Dr. Hampden, that he had "no authority against an Act of Parliament" and the royal supremacy over the Church.

This had the effect, as it were, of a *revelation* on the men of the Oxford movement. They began to see more clearly that the Church of England was, by its very constitution, simply a department of the State, and they saw moreover that this condition of things in the Church of England had continued all along, ever since the false step taken in the sixteenth century, when the English sovereign, with the full consent of the bishops, and by Act of Parliament, made himself head of the Church, and through his

Law Courts, "in all causes ecclesiastical as well
as civil, Supreme." A few years later, after
Newman had left the Church of England, this
same servitude of the Established Church to the
State was brought out, even more clearly, in the
decision of the Law Courts, on the *Gorham case*,
by which the doctrine of regeneration in baptism
was made an open question in the Church of
England. It was this *revelation* of the Royal
Supremacy in matters of doctrine and discipline
that led to Newman's secession, and to that of
his immediate disciples. It was the *revelation*,
in the *Gorham case*, that was the immediate
cause that led to the submission to the Church
of Archdeacon Manning, and of those who, like
the Wilberforces, Hope Scott, and a host of
others, became Catholics about the same time
as our Cardinal Archbishop. It was he who,
at that time, said: "The Gorham case is a
revelation to us; it has opened our eyes to the
false step made by the Church of England
under the Tudor settlement." When some
were deliberating what to do, whether to submit to the Pope, or to form a *Free Church* of
England, independent of the State, it was
Manning who spoke memorable words. "No,"
said he, "three hundred years ago we left a
good ship for a boat; I am not going to leave
a boat for a tub."

However, in 1841, the leaders of the movement had not got so far as to think of leaving
the Church of England. They still hoped.
Newman writes: "I thought that the Anglican
Church was tyrannised over by a mere party."
Their hope was that they might be able gradually to influence the Christian public opinion

of the country, and draw it to a desire of returning to *Primitive Christianity* and the *Church of the Fathers.*

They did not then see that the Catholic Church is the Visible Kingdom of God upon earth, essentially one, and visibly united in its Head—the Bishop of Rome, successor to St. Peter, whom Christ had made the centre of unity, and placed on that "chair of truth," against which He had declared "the gates of hell should not prevail."

Newman, eminently, and for long years, had made the history of the early centuries of Christianity the matter of his profound study. We, his disciples (for I came under the influence of his mind about 1839 or 1840) were directed by his writings into the same line of study. We knew that the Fathers, St. Athanasius, St. Leo, and the rest, whom we took as trustworthy witnesses of the faith of the Primitive Church, were the chief agents in preserving the Church from Arian, Nestorian, Eutychian, and other errors, especially by means of the General Councils, which expressed the infallible authority of the Church; and we saw that if it had not been for the perpetual indwelling of the Holy Spirit in the Church, it would have been impossible for the faith to have been preserved, amidst the revolts of rationalising Christians, Alexandrian Platonists and Jews, and hair-splitting Greek Sophists.

. But we saw no less clearly that the Church of England had become little more than a department of the State, and that it had helplessly abdicated all claim to an independent judgment in all matters of religious faith.

We perceived also, gradually, and we were helped to see it through Newman's supereminent knowledge of ecclesiastical history, that the Bishop of Rome had always been the supreme agent in keeping the whole Church united; in the Councils, also, he always had held the most prominent place, as well by his legates who presided, as by his sanction of their decrees; which were considered binding on the whole Church, only when they had received his approval.

Moreover, the more we read these early Christian writers, the more clearly did we see that, besides the doctrines which the Church of England held in common with Rome, nearly every doctrine which the English Refomation had rejected, was held to be part and parcel of the Christian faith, by those authorities of early Christianity—I mean such doctrines as the Real Presence and Sacrifice of the Mass, so clearly taught by St. Clement of Rome, who speaks of the "Eucharistic Offering to God," which has succeeded to the oblations at the altar in the Old Law. St. Ignatius of Antioch again says, speaking of certain heretics: "They abstain from the Eucharist and the Oblations, because they do not confess that the Eucharist is the Flesh of our Saviour Jesus Christ, the Flesh which suffered for our sins, which the Father in His mercy raised again," &c. St. Justin the martyr, and St. Irenæus, are equally explicit. Well do I remember the first time when, at Oxford, I read these and many similar testimonies, in the "Library of the Fathers," especially a long passage in the "Catechetical Instructions" of St. Cyril of Jerusalem, in which he says that "the bread and wine are changed into the Body and Blood of Christ, as truly as the water was changed into wine at the marriage of Cana in Galilee."

In short, we became convinced that, on these doctrines, as also on those of purgatory, prayers for the dead, the honour due to the Blessed Virgin and the Saints, and our right to ask their prayers, and last but not least, on the authority of the Pope; or, as St. Irenæus calls it, "the superior Headship of the Church, founded at Rome by SS. Peter and Paul, to which Church all Churches and all the faithful in the whole world were bound to have recourse, or to be united with it in communion"—we saw that the ancient Church and the Church of the Roman communion were substantially agreed.

These studies had led many of us to think seriously that it might be our duty, at once, to make our submission to the Catholic Church, which we saw had its centre in the Pope who, as it would seem, was, by divine institution, head of the visible Church.

Newman was not as yet convinced that the Roman supremacy over all Churches was a matter of divine institution. He thought it was in the Mind of our Lord in His words to Peter, as the normal condition of the Church; but he then supposed it was only *indirectly* of divine, but was *directly* of ecclesiastical institution. It was only in 1844, when he had reviewed all his studies, throughout more than fifteen years, of the Fathers and the Councils, and of the whole course of ecclesiastical history, that in the course of writing his "Essay on Development," he came to the conclusion that the supremacy of the

Pope was the key-stone of the arch, and that it was his own indispensable duty in conscience to submit himself to the Roman obedience.

Thus, as I have shown, a fundamental revolution had been taking place in our idea of the Church, and of Christianity. For the first time, the vision of the world-wide Church, in its majestic unity, had come before us. We saw it, for the first time, not as we had supposed it to be, an aggregate of congregations—a voluntary union of spiritual families, but as a world-wide essentially united kingdom—the Kingdom, as shown to the Prophet Daniel, like to a stone cut from a mountain without hand, set up by the God of heaven, which was to be gradually developed until it became a mountain filling the whole earth, destined to last for ever. Of this world-wide Church, we knew the Church of England was once a portion. How it could form any part of that unity, since its separation 300 years before, we could not see.

From the moment that we were convinced that the charges against the Roman communion, of being idolatrous, anti-Christian, and the rest, had been answered, they were completely banished from our minds. The fact that it formed the vast majority of Catholic Christendom, necessarily took away the chief ground of our Protestant position. Sides were changed; we saw that we had to defend our *protest*, or else yield to the authority we had protested against.

But Newman and others of our leaders had not, as yet, come to this point. They thought Rome was right in claiming the headship of the Church; but they also considered that a legitimate claim may be pushed too far. They

E

reflected that there had been abuses in the Papal relations with England, in old times; demands for large money payments, and for the grant of the incomes of English Bishoprics and other rich benefices, in favour of Italian ecclesiastics, which had been a grievance, in old times, against which English Catholic sovereigns had uniformly protested.

These, and other things had led, first to a coolness on the part of the English towards Rome, in Catholic times, and this had grown up, especially, during the days of the anti-popes, when rival Pontiffs each claimed the obedience of Catholics, and the justice of the claim of each was so open to doubt, that England embraced the obedience of one Pope, France and Scotland of another, and Spain at one time owned the authority of a third claimant. In fact, the contention between the popes and anti-popes was, to a great extent, a battle of rival nationalities.

Such historical difficulties, and many others, helped to complicate the question, and the result was that the most of us resolved to stay by Newman; doubting the soundness of our own conclusions to which, with far greater knowledge, he had not arrived.

Three of us younger men, however, went off and were received into the Catholic Church; and it is somewhat singular that these three men were Scotsmen, Johnstone Grant, of St. John's College, now a Jesuit; Edward Douglas, of Christ Church, now a Redemptorist; and his friend Scott-Murray, squire of Danesfield, deceased. I was soon to be another Scotsman added to the list. I suppose our coming from

Jacobite and Scotch Episcopalian stocks, and
not being so rooted as Englishmen are, in favour
of everything English, left us freer to criticise
and condemn Church of England Christianity.
Our secession was decided by several things:
The publication by Newman of *Tract* 90, the
object of which was to show that there was no
need to go to Rome, because we found nearly all
Roman doctrines were taught in the Primitive
Church, although rejected or neglected by the
Church of England; because the 39 Articles were
not articles of faith, but an attempt at compromise.
They were intended to include Puritans. and
Catholics who were ready to give up the Pope!
This confirmed our growing convictions—our
disgust with the Church of England was all but
complete, and it only increased this disgust, if it
could be shown that her founders had deliberate-
ly ventured to obscure the old religion, by what
Newman had called "the stammering words of
ambiguous formularies."

The *Tract* made a great stir throughout the
University and the country; but, as every one
knows, the interpretation of the *Articles* was
furiously repudiated by the Anglican bishops,
and by the Protestant public-opinion of the
country. The bigotry and intolerance of the
Puritan party was stirred to a white heat.
Newman saw that his attempt to find terms of
reconciliation, and to speak of the creed of
Rome as substantially identical, differing only
on minor points, from Primitive Christianity,
with which the Anglican Church professed to
agree—had failed. But the truth has proclaimed
itself trumpet-tongued throughout the English-
speaking world.

It has in our day come to be admitted by all. It is now more than twenty years since I copied the following passage from the *Saturday Review*, no friend, as we know, to Catholics, nor to the Catholicising movement in the Church of England: "The distinctive principle of the English Reformation was an appeal to Christian antiquity, as admirable, and probably as imaginary, as the 'Golden Age' of the poets. The era of the Protestant Reformation was before the age of accurate historical criticism. The true method of historical criticism was as yet uncreated, and it is not too much to say, that whatever accurate knowledge we now possess of the Church of the first centuries, has been obtained within the last fifty years, and that a better acquaintance with the remains of antiquity has convinced us that many doctrines and practices, which have been commonly accounted to be peculiarities of later Romanism, existed in the best and purest ages of Christianity."

No one could ignore Newman's part in this remarkable change in public opinion, and in the historical judgment of educated men of whatever creed, or of no creed at all. It is this which Cardinal Manning expresses, when he says. "The designer and editor of the 'Library of the Fathers,' has planted himself on the undivided Church of the first six centuries of Christianity: and he holds the field. The key of the position is lost." The old Anglican claim to hold a *via media* on the basis of Christian antiquity, between Catholic Christendom on the one side, and Protestantism on the other, has been for ever exploded.

The second thing which hastened my submis-

sion to the Catholic Church was the reading of a
Catholic book, Milner's "End of Controversy."
Some years before I had taken the book away
from my friend Johnstone Grant, to whom it had
been given by a Catholic priest in London. I
rated him soundly for reading a Catholic work,
told him he had no more right to read it than to
study a Socinian or Infidel book. The book lay
in my drawer in college.

Newman's sermons and Pusey's writings on
baptismal grace and post-baptismal sin had
wrought in me a moral revolution, and a terrible
fear that I had lost God for ever. I saw myself
a baptized Christian and, therefore, once "a
temple of God." But through the sins of childhood and of thoughtless youth, reduced to a state
in which I could not doubt that I had lost the
grace of God, and my soul had become a
dwelling-place of devils. Anglican theology
taught clearly, in its Prayer Book and Catechism
almost as clearly as it is taught in the Catholic
Catechism, that souls are regenerated in Baptism.
But it tells of no other Sacrament by which sins
committed after Baptism may be remitted. At
that day, no one thought of proving the belief of
the Church of England in the Sacrament of
Penance, Confession, and Priestly Absolution,
from the few words about the absolving power
in the Anglican *ordination service*, and in that
for the *visitation of the sick*. Any one who
wishes to do so, may find the doctrine there. I
had never heard of it, until, in an hour of deep
mental distress, I turned over the pages of
Milner's End of Controversy. There I first heard
of the Sacrament of reconciliation after post-
baptismal sin, and it was *Milner* that sent me

to the Anglican Prayer Book, for proof that the Church of England admitted, in theory, the same doctrine on this point which had always and everywhere been, not only taught, but practised in the Catholic Church.

This discovery was a great relief to my mind, but it did not increase my confidence in the Church of England. There were the "stammering words of ambiguous formularies" once more. What was to be said of a Church which had so obscured a divine ordinance for the remission of sin—a Sacrament therefore, by its own definition; to quote the words of the Catechism : "A Sacrament is an outward and visible sign of an inward and spiritual grace given to us ; ordained by Christ Himself, as a *means* whereby we receive the same, and a pledge to assure us thereof."

Here then was a Sacrament, so necessary for salvation, which had practically fallen into complete disuse in the Church of England for 300 years !

It was difficult to try Confession in the Anglican Church. However, I made the attempt, as at least a moral discipline. Archdeacon Manning, whom I knew, was in Oxford, for it was his turn to preach the University sermon. I went to Confession to him in Merton College Chapel, his own college. It was a relief to me for a time. He also gave me excellent advice, and, I think, counselled me to put myself under Newman, and try to remain and take Orders in the Anglican Church. I tried to do so. I was admitted, by Newman's great kindness, as one of his first companions at Littlemore. I remained with him about a year. The life was something like what we had read of in the "Lives of the

Fathers of the Desert"—of prayer, fasting, and
study. We rose at midnight to recite the
Nocturnal office of the Roman Breviary. I
remember, direct invocation of Saints was
omitted, and, instead, we asked God that the
Saint of the day might pray for us. I think we
passed an hour in private prayer, and, for the
first time, I learned what *meditation* meant. We
fasted every day till twelve, and in Lent and
Advent till five. There was some mitigation on
Sundays and the greater festivals. We went to
Communion at the village church and to the
service there, morning and evening, every day;
we went to Confession every week. Once after
Confession I said to Newman, "Are you sure you
have the power of giving absolution?" He
paused, and then said in a tone of deep distress,
"Why will you ask me? Ask Pusey." This
was, I think, in the spring of 1843. It was the
first indication I had received that Newman had
begun seriously to doubt his position in the
Anglican Church. I see from his "Apologia"
that his doubts as to whether the Church of
Rome was not altogher in the right, and the
Church of England wholly in the wrong, had
taken root in his mind about that time.

I had promised him, soon after going to
Littlemore, that I would stay three years. He
had made it a condition. I gave the promise,
but after a year I found it impossible to keep it.
With great grief I left my dear master, and made
my submission to the Catholic Church. My
secession led to Newman's resigning his parish.
His last sermon, as an Anglican, was preached
at Littlemore. It is entitled "The Parting of
Friends." He thought he was compromised by

my act, and he was much displeased with me for breaking my promise.

After two years, he and his other companions at Littlemore were received into the Church.

We left the Church of England with grief. All the good we knew, we had learned there; we had been led step by step by God's grace, but we left, because we could not close our eyes to the fact that the Church of England was no part of the Visible Church; rather than separate from which Sir Thomas More, Bishop Fisher, and hundreds of others have laid down their lives in martyrdom.

Almost the first thing Newman did after his reception into the Church was to take the trouble to come all the way to Ratcliffe College, in Leicestershire, where I was studying, to see me, in order to show that he blamed me no longer. A year after I was ordained priest I went to see him, when he was living in community with Father Faber, Dalgairns and others at St. Wilfrid's in Staffordshire. They had all been ordained. I remember he *would* serve my Mass, as an act of humility and affection. Since that time I have always paid him an annual visit at the Oratory, Birmingham, where he always received me with the most cordial affection. When I first went to Rome, as representative there of my Order, (that of the Fathers of Charity, founded by Rosmini,) he gave me, as Cardinal, a letter to the Pope. This introduction has been, for the last eight years, of great service to me in Rome.

Soon after Easter of this year I paid him my last visit. He sent for me to come to him, before he rose in the morning, saying that after dressing, he might feel too much exhausted to receive me. I found him weak, weak indeed, in body, but as bright and clear in mind as ever. I told him news from Rome which I knew would interest him. He listened with all his old intensity of thought: fully appreciated the facts and the situation of matters ecclesiastical and political.

I knelt down; took his hand, and kissed it. I felt sure I should not see him again. I thanked him for all the good he had done me, since, under God, he had been, as I hoped, the instrument of my salvation. I asked his blessing, which he gave me with great earnestness, simplicity, and tenderness. Three months later I stood by his bier.

O, great and holy soul, remember us with God, and may our prayers and Masses avail to thine eternal rest and peace!

Possibilities and difficulties of Reunion.

A REVIEW

OF

DR. PUSEY'S EIRENICON.

BY

WILLIAM LOCKHART, B.A., Oxon,

PRIEST OF THE DIOCESE OF WESTMINSTER.

REPRINTED FROM THE SECOND EDITION OF 1866.

PREFACE

TO

THE SECOND EDITION.

THE FOLLOWING REVIEW contains the substance of two papers which originally appeared in the "Weekly Register," and were afterwards reprinted.

The first of the two letters from Dr. Pusey, which will be found in the Appendix, was addressed to that journal after the appearance of the earlier portion of the "Review," which accounts for the subsequent references to it.

In putting out a second edition of my "Review," I wish to deprecate the charge of presumption that might be brought against me, if it were supposed that I had ventured on untrodden ground, in the favourable view I have formed of the possibility or even reality of some kind of corporate movement towards reunion in the Anglican Church.

In nothing that I have said do I think that I have gone beyond that beaten track, in which I have intended only to follow the footsteps of the venerated Cardinal Wiseman, in his memorable Letter to Lord Shrewsbury, written more than twenty years ago, the principles of which I have good reasons to know he never retracted.

In 1841, six months after the appearance of Tract 90, he speaks of "the facilities for the reunion of England to the Catholic Church beyond what have before existed." Further on he declares that "no one who has the means of judging can doubt that the feelings which have been expressed in favour of a return to unity by the Anglican Church are every day widely spreading and deeply sinking." Again: "The sooner an end be put to the present painful position of the Anglican Church with relation to the rest of the world the better. We may depend upon a willing, an able, and a most zealous coöperation with any effort we may make towards bringing her into her rightful position in Catholic unity with the Holy See and the Churches of its obedience; in other words, with the Church Catholic. Is this a visionary idea? Is it merely the expression of a strong desire? I know that many will so judge it; perhaps *were I to consult my own quiet, I would not venture to express it.* But I will with simplicity of heart cling to hopefulness, cheered, as I feel it, by so many promising appearances. . . . The return of this country, through its Established Church, to Catholic unity, would put an end to religious dissent and interior feud, I feel no doubt."

Such were the late Cardinal's views on the possibilities of the Anglican movement twenty-five years ago, and he was not discouraged on account of the obvious difficulties which would have to be overcome. He continues: "The enemy of good will not allow an end to be put to dissentions and disunion without strong and repeated efforts to prevent it. . . . In addition to this, there will be sincere scruples about particular practices, unwillingness to surrender certain forms, complicated questions of hierarchical arrangements, orders, clerical discipline, and many others which it is needless to anticipate, because they will soon enough show themselves."

In all that I have written, I feel sure that I have not only not exceeded, but have kept far within the limits which the Cardinal allowed himself. I am not half as sanguine that now, in 1866, the Established Church is moving towards the centre of unity, as his Eminence was in 1841, notwithstanding that the Catholic movement within the Establishment is so much more pronounced, and so much more widely spread, than when he wrote twenty-five years ago.

Of course, no one can say for certain that the Anglican establishment, as a corporate body, may not eventually be drawn into the movement. If this were to take place, it would be hardly more wonderful than the doctrinal advance that has been made in the Anglican body during the past twenty years. A great deal may depend on political events, and on the kind of bishops that the chief minister of the Crown may be willing, and may venture, to nominate. I think, however, that he would be a bold prophet who would predict from any signs now discoverable, that such an event is advancing on our horizon.

What I do think all must discern is, that everywhere throughout the Anglican Church and its colonial offshoots there is a movement tending to the disintegration of the National Church, and of Anglicanism, as a combination of elements which of their nature cannot amalgamate, and which cannot remain together in solution, when once they have passed into a condition of activity. I cannot help thinking, however, that within the seething mass of Anglicanism there may exist elements for new combinations, and that not improbably a Free Church of England may be elaborated, in which great numbers of earnest minds may find a temporary home; those, namely, who though deeply possessed with a love of revealed truth, and holding in theory the principle of all dogma in a belief in the infallible authority of the Church, have not as yet come to see that the whole edifice of revealed truth was made by our Lord to hold together and rest on him, who received for himself and his successors the name and office of the Rock, or immovable basis on which that Church was founded, which is itself "the pillar and ground of the truth."

It has, then, been my desire to guide myself in what I have written on the possibility of corporate reunion, by principles which have been laid down by one who was a great light in the Church of our age, who was large-minded, large-hearted, and far-seeing, if sometimes in his ardent charity he may perhaps have been too sanguine of immediate results. That I have done justice to the meaning of my author in my " Review " of the " Eirenicon," I have his own express testimony, and that I have done this, though in a cordial spirit, yet without saying anything *male sonans*, I think I may conclude from the words of the learned writer in the " Études Religieuses " (the organ of the French Jesuits), in which he feels justified in calling my " Review " a *chef d'œuvre*— words which I am not vain enough to think appropriate, except inasmuch as they must at least imply that I have expressed myself not un-

becomingly on open questions, and have written
nothing *"offensive to pious ears."*

I believe it has been felt by some, for whose
opinion I entertain great reverence, that the line
I have taken, in dwelling on the possibility of a
corporate movement towards reunion is mistaken
if not mischievous at the present day, as tending
to divert the minds of Anglicans who have strong
misgivings on the tenability of their position from
boldly confronting this question, and as fostering
a delusion, as if the Church could ever recede
from any principle for the sake of unity. I think
I have said enough on these subjects in my
"Review," which I need not here repeat, but to
obviate misunderstanding, I wish, in the first
place, to express my conviction that the author
of the "Eirenicon," and those who think with him,
have not thus far advanced beyond what is called
the "branch theory," of the Church—a theory
which they could not retain either as individuals
or as a body on entering Catholic communion,
so that there is no question at present of individual submission. Supposing, however, that they
hold this theory conscientiously, it is one on
which they may also hold almost every Catholic
doctrine, except that of the Divine authority of the
Holy See; but there is surely reason to hope that
as dogmatic truth develops in their minds, and
is operative on their lives, they will in the same
proportion be drawn towards the Rock of Peter,
whether as individuals or as a body, as men
drink of the waters of a river of which they trace
the stream until they reach its source high up in
the primeval rock.

Hence, it appears to me that, while the authorities of the Church are bound to hold forth no

F

delusive hopes, and have simply to enunicate in
an unmistakable way the terms of Catholic
communion, which are incompatible with the
theory of branch churches, this by no means
excludes such expressions of private opinion as
I have ventured on, as to the possible workings
of this very theory, under the pressure of the
present circumstances of Anglicanism, into such
a view of the Church as might serve for a basis of
negotiations for reunion. For there can be, I
conceive, no question that should it ever happen
that any large number of Anglicans were to come
forward as a body declaring that they were ready
to accept, in some sense recognized among us,
the Catholic doctrine of the Church and its Head,
our authorities would be disposed to meet such
a body on the principle that reunion on any
terms which the Holy See could allow would be
better than perpetuated schism.

To Catholics who are such, because they know
and submit to the infallible teaching of the Visible
Church, it is no doubt a difficulty to understand
the position of advanced Anglicans, which seems
to them so illogical; but the order of ideas is one
thing, the order of facts is another, and if we
who are converts will look back on our past
religious history, we shall, I believe, generally
find that we accepted each Catholic doctrine
gradually and by itself, and last of all came to
the belief in the Church and its Head on which
all really depends. The same process of thought
seems going on amongst Anglicans as a body.
When sincere minds have arrived at a certain
point, submission becomes an imperative duty,
and when large numbers of minds are acting and
reacting on one another in the same direction, and

in the same order of ideas, I do not see why the result should not be the submission of a body. This is what I mean by a corporate movement. Whether that movement shall end in the submission of individuals as so many separate units, or of those individuals as an aggregate body, will depend on a number of circumstances. But there can be no question of the importance of such a corporate union, if we admit its possibility, and this for many reasons, especially since there will always be vast numbers of minds that would go with the crowd who would not have sufficient self-reliance or clearness of conviction to go alone.

It may, indeed, be argued, that, supposing such a movement to be going on, there will always be some individuals whose ideas are in advance of their contemporaries, which is only saying that there must be leaders to every party, and that these persons would possibly be endangering their own souls while they were waiting to bring others on. To this I would reply, that conviction is a thing of gradual growth, made up of many indefinable influences; of this Dr. Newman's history of his own mind in the "Apologia" is an example. It seldom happens that a man rises a sound Anglican in the morning, and goes to bed a no less sound Catholic. It is true that a hundred influences adverse to Divine grace are always at work around us, but I cannot believe that any sincere man would be permitted to be so influenced by the connections of party as to make shipwreck of duty and of faith, as it were, at the very entrance of the harbour; but, supposing such a case possible, I more than doubt if all which could be said about the duty of individual submission to known truth would have the effect of preventing so great an evil. Holding, then, as I do with the late Cardinal, that a great corporate movement is actually going on, and that corporate reunion is a possibility, I am making no new suggestion in speaking of it, but am only discussing contingencies which must be as clearly before the minds of Anglicans as before my own. Neither am I in any way answerable for the possible misuse which individuals here and there may make of my words. The mercy of God to sinners is a great truth. but some may (and doubtless do) pervert this doctrine to their own destruction. And so the corporate reunion of the Anglican Church may be the will of God, and yet there may be some who have come or may come to a point of conviction where individual submission is their plain duty, a necessary sacrifice to the exigence of truth.

Meanwhile, one can hardly fail to recognise a manifest providence in the phenomena which we at present witness, of large numbers of Anglicans, whom it would be gross uncharity to pronounce insincere, being led on step by step till they come to accept almost every Catholic doctrine, and yet not coming, as it would appear, till at the last, to realise that one doctrine of the Divine authority of the Holy See, which when once accepted would make their position one of formal or conscious schism. For it is surely obvious that the leaders of the party, as long as they remain where they are in *good faith*, are doing a work which humanly speaking could be done in no other way. Fully believing in their own priesthood, they are teaching by learned and devout writings, and from the pulpits of the Anglican Church, and with all the prestige of their position, nearly every Catholic doctrine, and celebrating what they believe to be the Mass with all the externals of Catholic ritual, and multitudes are learning from them what, on account of early prejudice, they would not accept from our lips, even if we had the means and opportunity of reaching them.

As for the terms of communion, I suppose there is no question of any other than those which have been laid down by the Council of Trent.* To this the Church is bound ; from this

* Perhaps the most remarkable feature of the movement is, that the ancient antipathy to Rome, and contented isolation, of Anglicanism, seem to have wellnigh passed away amongst the advanced school of Anglicans, and have been succeeded by deep aspirations towards the centre of unity. The *Eirenicon* itself, with its ten editions, and the reception it has met with amongst the different schools in the English Church, is one proof of this. The same is borne out by such statements as we quote from a leading High Church organ, the *Christian Remembrancer*, speaking on the Thirty-nine Articles. . . . " In the times that are coming on the Church of England, the question will arise, What service have the Articles of the Church of England ever done ? and what use are they at the present day ? But we venture to go a step beyond this volume (the *Eirenicon*) and boldly proclaim our opinion, that before union with Rome can be effected, the Thirty-nine Articles must be wholly withdrawn. They are virtually withdrawn at the present moment."

Again, quite lately, at a crowded meeting of the English Church Union at Willis's Rooms, on a vote of thanks to the author for his *Eirenicon*, which was afterwards carried by acclamation, an amendment was she cannot recede ; more than this she does not require. The dogmatic decrees of the Council being taken as the basis, there will be room for any explanations, or concessions on non-essentials, that the authorities of the Church might think it just and prudent to grant in order to render the work of reunion easier.

proposed, "that the Council of Trent could not be accepted as a basis of reunion," on which the proposer and seconder found themselves, with one other person, forming the minority. On this occasion Dr. Pusey spoke as follows. We quote from the *Guardian* of June 20, 1866 :—

Dr. Pusey (who rose amidst enthusiastic cheers) said— It would not be right at this late hour to dwell on what Mr. Gurney has stated with regard to the meaning of the *Eirenicon*. I would beg, however, to remark that he has omitted one exceedingly important word. That is the word "explained." (Cheers.) What I have said, what I have stated to Gallican Bishops, and what they have clearly understood, was this—that I believe the Council of Trent, whatever its look was, and our Articles, whatever their look was, could be so explained as to reconcile one with the other. (Cheers.) Of course there is a mode of explaining the Council of Trent which I could not receive ; and if it simply went forth that this Society was committed to the *Eirenicon*, and the *Eirenicon* to reunion on the basis of the Council of Trent, it would give both a wrong explanation of the *Eirenicon*, and a wrong interpretation of the meaning of this Association. (Cheers.) When Mr. Gurney began his amendment I was very much inclined to second it. (Laughter.) The *Eirenicon* is a thick book, and there is no reason why this Society should commit itself to it. But what the amendment means is the real object of the *Eirenicon*. When I began to write it, nothing was farther from my purpose of writing. It was put to me;

" You must answer this letter of Dr. Manning"—as he then was—and I undertook the task because it was laid upon me by those whom I could not refuse. When I had got through a good deal of our defence, it came suddenly to me—not from myself—" Is this all? Is it to end in this? Is there to be this continual division and separation?" And then I wrote the rest. Afterwards I went abroad in order to ascertain whether what I hoped for was a dream or whether it was reality. Of course I cannot repeat anything of which I am unable to speak. I saw various Bishops, and some that the papers did not know that I saw. (A laugh.) I saw also theologians whom the papers happily know nothing about; and I went with them through all the details of our case. I stated what our difficulties were—how we believed that they could be explained, and how we believed that they could be met. I assure you that people in England will be extremely astonished if I am able to show (as I hope soon to do) how much that is popularly supposed to be *de fide* with Roman Catholics is not *de fide* with them. (Cheers.) I will only give one instance. I saw a theologian, and one of the most eminent. We talked for two hours about the Council of Trent, and about our belief, as it is expressed by those whom we considered to be the most genuine sons of the Church of England. The result was that point after point he was satisfied; and the interview ended in his saying, "I shall salute you as a true brother." (Loud cheers.)

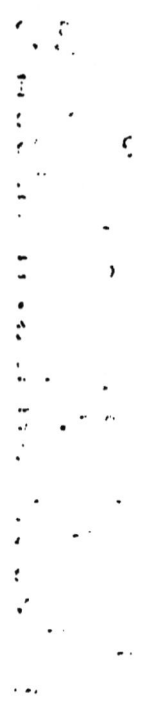

A REVIEW

OF

DR. PUSEY'S EIRENICON.*

IT is quite conceivable that two Catholic readers might rise from a perusal of this book with totally opposite views as to its character and aim. To one it might seem what its name implies, an olive-branch of peace, to the other a firebrand; to the one a hopeful move in the direction of faith and unity, to the other a work calculated to strengthen and perpetuate the wall of separation between Anglicans and the Catholic Church. For the work has a twofold object indicated by its double title. It is, on the one hand, a controversial defence of the Church of England as a portion of the visible Church; and yet it is, on the other hand, a most distinct admission throughout of the shortcomings of Anglicanism, of its abnormal condition as separated from the centre of unity, and is, perhaps, the most unequivocal advance that has ever been made

* *The Church of England a Portion of Christ's Holy Catholic Church, and a Means of Restoring Visible Unity: an Eirenicon.* In a Letter to the Author of "The Christian Year." By E. B. PUSEY, D.D., Regius Professor of Hebrew, and Canon of Christ Church, Oxford. Oxford: Parker. 1865.

towards negotiation for healing the schism of the
sixteenth century. For myself, while deploring
a good deal of the controversial portion, and
thinking that more intercourse with Catholics
would have saved Dr. Pusey from much misunderstanding of our doctrine, yet on the whole
I venture to believe that the book ought to be
accepted by Catholics as an Eirenicon, according
to its author's expressed intention. We make
every allowance for an envoy who comes to us
from the hostile camp, bearing an olive-branch
in one hand, even though he carries a sword in
the other; and we do not roughly repel him, even
though he claims to speak only in the name of
one division of the enemy, and though his pro-
posals are not of unconditional surrender, but
of conference and negotiation.

No doubt, one might take another line, and
urge the inconsistency of the Anglican position,
and the special inconsistency of Dr. Pusey in
remaining in the Church of England, after his
declarations in 1850 and the events which have
since occurred. It is, indeed, difficult to understand how he can speak of the Anglican Church
as having any authoritative voice, or being in
any way a Divine teacher, or having any mind
or moral personality at all. The best that can
be said of it even by its ablest defenders is (to
quote the words of a contemporary), "that if it
tolerates heresy, it also tolerates orthodoxy, and
that its Prayer-book and formularies admit an
orthodox sense." Catholics, in fact, can see in it
nothing but a mere compromise between two
contending parties, bound over before the civil
magistrate under heavy penalties to keep the
peace and live together. This and a great deal

more may be fully admitted; nevertheless, when:
all has been said, there remains the fact that
numbers of learned and apparently earnest men
do not see their inconsistency, now in 1865, any
more than their predecessors, the leaders of the
movement twenty years ago, and who are now
Catholics, saw their inconsistency in 1840.

Old Catholics who have watched both movements cannot see less reason for confidence now
than formerly. They cannot see that the celebrated Gorham judgment, or any of the later
decisions in the law courts, have changed the
status of the Church of England. Those who
could believe in the Church of England, in spite
of the original establishment of the royal supremacy, are not necessarily insincere or more
unreasonable, if they believe in it, in spite of the
acts of that supremacy. In 1840 it was main-
tained by the leaders of the movement that the
Church of England, though well-nigh disabled
by the incubus of the supremacy, was still alive;
in 1865 their successors only maintain the same.
Nor is it as the case would be, if from the time
when Newman, Manning, and other leaders of
the Anglican school left the English Church, the
Catholic movement had come to an end, or become
insignificant. On the contrary, the appearance
of such a work as Dr. Pusey's, and from one in
his eminent position, is only one amongst a
hundred evidences, that the movement, far from
having come to an end, has become broader and
deeper. It cannot be denied that almost every
Catholic doctrine is now preached in hundreds
of Anglican pulpits—not after the tentative
manner of the original Tractarian movement, but
boldly and distinctly, indicating unmistakably.

that the leaders are conscious that they are speaking to a laity sufficiently imbued with Catholic ideas to understand and sympathise with their teachers. In nothing is this change, from the reserve then necessary to the explicitness now possible, more marked than in the restoration in so many churches of the Catholic vestments, as a natural embodiment of the unequivocal teaching of the Eucharistic Sacrifice.

It has been objected to Dr. Pusey's book that its aim is not so much the restoration of unity, as the prevention of individual conversion. It certainly may have this effect in some cases, and this may have been in part his object; but we can hardly blame him for doing what he could not be sincere if he did not do. The same was done by Dr. Manning and Dr. Newman, so long as they believed in the Anglican position, and would be done by any one honestly in error. Once let us admit that Dr. Pusey believes, strange and unaccountable as it may seem to us, that the Anglican position is tenable, and we shall see that he could not act differently. But what hope, it may be said, can there be of this reunion, while Anglicans sincerely hold what they do, since the Church cannot change her essential doctrine? What result can be hoped for, what course is there but that of individual conversion from error to truth, and how can corporate reunion be possible except by the conversion of each individual of the separated body? I cannot, of course, profess in a short review to answer all the difficulties that may be raised on this matter of corporate reunion; yet corporate reunion cannot be impossible, since it has been realised by the Church, at the Council of Florence, as well as in

various other transactions with separated bodies.
There can be no doubt that in such negotiations
for reunion on the part of separatists there must
always have been much that was unsatisfactory
and anomalous, much previous inconsistency of
statement, much of indecision and uncertainty of
action.* The history of the Council of Florence
affords an instance of this. What must have been
the inconsistency of many of the Oriental Bishops,
who had acted for years out of communion with
Rome, and defended their position even in the
Council itself, and yet afterwards submitted to
all that Rome required as terms of communion?
Of course I am not comparing the present informal
movement in the Anglican Church with any of
these, but only observing that inconsistency on
the part of separatists is perhaps almost involved
in the idea of negotiation for corporate reunion;
and yet this has not prevented the Church from
admitting such inchoate measures in the direction
of unity. The failure of the Council of Florence
to effect a permanent reunion is obviously no
argument against the principle, or it would prove
too much, namely, that the Church erred in
attempting it. But if the Church attempted it,
clearly the principle is sound; that it failed of
success is to be attributed to the evil will of man,
which has so often marred the fair purpose of
GOD. Besides, other corporate reunions have
been attempted, before and since, and have
succeeded; such as that of the Armenians under

* Since the appearance of my first edition this point
has been dwelt on with great force by Dr. Pusey's reviewer
in the "Études Religieuses" (Feb. 1866), the organ of the
French Jesuits.

Eugenius IV., and of other Oriental sects, some
of which have taken place even in our own day.
To turn now to the work itself. Dr. Pusey
begins his book with what he calls a personal
explanation; he had wished to abstain from controversy for the remainder of his life, but his
friends considered that he was in some measure
bound to reply to Archbishop Manning's published
letter; and this required something controversial
in his answer. He goes on to defend himself
from a charge made by the Archbishop, that in
fraternising with the Low Church party in certain
protests against the Rationalistic school in the
Church of England, he had been " drifting back
from the old moorings." He says : " Ever since
I knew them (which was not in my earliest years),
I have loved those who are called Evangelicals ;
I loved them because they loved our Lord ; I
loved them for their zeal for souls. I often
thought them narrow, yet I was drawn to individuals amongst them, more than to others
who held truths in common with myself which
the Evangelicals did not hold, at least explicitly.
When occasion came, as in some of our troubles
at Oxford, we acted together. . . . . . I have
united with the Evangelicals now as I did before,
whenever they would join with me in defence of
our common faith. I have not united with them
in any of those things which were not in ac-
cordance with my own principles. . . . . . And
this perhaps may be an occasion to mention
what relates to a very sacred season of my life
when death seemed day by day nearer. Had it
so pleased God that I should then die, I should
have worded the confession of my faith in words
like these : ' I believe *explicitly* all which I know

God to have revealed to His Church, and *implicitly*
anything if He has revealed it, which I know
not; in simple words, I believe all which the
Church believes: this is my habit of mind now,
this I confess when I say to God, "I believe one
Holy Catholic and Apostolic Church."'" Dr.
Pusey goes on to comment on Dr. Manning's
Letter, of which he says the real point is to assert
the contradictory of the statement that "the
Church of England is in God's hand the great
bulwark against infidelity in this land." To
defend this proposition is one of his principal
objects throughout his book. He explains, however, the sense in which he understood the
proposition to have been originally enunciated
by Dr. Newman.* He says, "This saying was
not mine, but that of one of the deepest thinkers
and observers in the Roman Communion. It
relates plainly only to a present fact; it does not
aver that the Church of England is the best
possible bulwark, but only as a matter of fact
that it is at this moment, in God's Providence,
a real and chief bulwark against infidelity. Of
course any Roman Catholic must think that the
Roman Communion, if it were of the same extent
in this land as the English Church is now, would
be a much stronger bulwark, but this is not the
question." He goes on to show what has been
the estimate formed of the Church of England,
in its relation to Catholic doctrine and the hopes
of reunion, by illustrious Catholics in other days.
"We are not in most things," says Dupin to

---

* See *Dr. Newman's Letter*, in the Appendix, in which
he expresses a decided approval of the line taken in this
paper. His own estimate of the *Eirenicon* has been
since expressed in his Letter to Dr. Pusey.

Archbishop Wake, "so far removed from one another that we may not be mutually reconciled." "This union," says Dr. Doyle (Bishop of Kildare and Leighlin, the celebrated "J. K. L."), "is not so difficult as appears to many. It is not difficult, for in the discussions which were held on this subject, in which Archbishop Wake was engaged, as in others which were carried on between Bossuet and Leibnitz, it appeared that the points of agreement between the Churches were numerous, those on which the parties hesitated few, and apparently not the most important. The effort which was then made was not attended with success, but its failure was owing more to Princes than to Priests, more to State policy than to a difference of belief."

The next thirty or forty pages contain an elaborate proof, drawn chiefly from the celebrated Tract 90 of Dr. Newman, that the Articles of the Church of England and the Decrees of Trent may be reconciled, and that there is nothing in the Decrees of Trent which may not be so interpreted as to form the basis of negotiation for the reunion of Anglicans to the Catholic Church. "We have been wont," Dr. Pusey says, "to dwell with pleasure on the amount of faith which we confess in common with the Roman Church. In the three creeds we confess together the whole doctrine as to the Holy Trinity and the Incarnation of our Blessed Lord; we teach alike, the one end of man, the resurrection of the body, the judgment according to the works, the life everlasting, and the everlasting fire." *

* Dr. Pusey's view on this point is remarkably borne out by an able and candid writer in the (Dissenting) *British Quarterly* for April, 1866.

Dr. Pusey goes on to maintain that the Anglican Church teaches with the Catholic Church regeneration in baptism, confession and absolution, the Real Presence and the Eucharistic Sacrifice, and has the same doctrine on grace and justification. The substance of a great deal which follows is, that, according to the view of the learned writer, there is nothing in the formal statements of the Church of England, in her Prayer-book, articles, and homilies, which cannot be reconciled with the formal statements of the Catholic Church.

On the question of the Church's unity, Dr. Pusey would hold an opinion differing, on important points, from the doctrine universally held by Catholics; *and here we fear would be the chief difficulty in discovering a common basis for negotiation.* He would look upon the Church as indissolubly one, by reason of a Sacramental bond of union, established between our Lord and all those who hold a right faith concerning Him, through the instrumentality of a rightly-ordained Priesthood. He appears to hold, that visible unity under one Head, and that Head the Bishop of Rome, is not only desirable, but according to the will and intention of our Lord; that any breach of this unity could not take place without sin, but that there may be such a thing as justifiable or material schism; and he would consider the separation of England from the Chair of Peter to be something of this nature. He writes: " This unity, derived from our Blessed Lord as Head of the Church, is imparted primarily through the Sacraments. ' All that were baptised into Christ have put on Christ, and having put Him on are one in Christ; all in the Holy'

G

Eucharist are one bread and one body who are partakers of that one Bread.' Unknown in face, in place separate, different in language, opposed, alas! in some things to one another, still before the throne of God they are One Holy Catholic Apostolic Church. This," he continues, "is sometimes called objective unity ; and this Divine gift requires, as a corresponding duty, what has been called subjective unity, or a unison of wills ; and of this intercommunion is the natural expression. But is all unity forfeited where the unity of intercommunion is suspended ? No one in the face of Church history can or does maintain, that all interruptions of intercommunion destroy unity. In the second century, the East, says Epiphanius, differing from the West, they received not from each other tokens of peace. In the next century was a temporary severance between Rome and both Asiatic and African Churches, through the Bishop of Rome, concerning whom St. Firmilian says: 'While thinking that all may be excommunicated by him, he excommunicated himself alone from all.' 'St. Meletius, of Antioch, though out of communion with Rome, presided at the second General Council, and after his death was owned to be a Saint by those who, in his lifetime, owned him not to be a Bishop.' The fifth General Council was the occasion of a schism which rent the West, Africa, Upper Italy, from East to West, and even Ireland ; nor was the schism wholly healed for a hundred and fifty years."

Such appears to be a very fair statement of the Anglican theory of the Church's unity. It is given here without comment, as a clear expression of what learned Anglicans think they have to say for their position. And for the same reason a careful perusal of the whole work may be recommended to those whose duty it is to be ready to answer difficulties. I do not recommend it to any but learned Catholics. As it is the work of one who has made Church history and the writings of the Holy Fathers the study of a lifetime, the controversial portion, based chiefly on the *writer's view* of the Patristic teaching, may easily present difficulties which an unlearned reader may not be able to answer. The Catholic theologian, who studies the Holy Fathers and historians of the early centuries, has a clue to guide him, in the perpetual unbroken tradition of the living Church, which is altogether wanting to the Anglican student, however learned. Anglicans study the Fathers much as the ordinary Protestant studies Holy Scripture; without the clue they wander hither and thither through a labyrinth, disappointed and baffled at every turn; or, after seeming to have found the road, they may chance to discover that the shortest course is to retrace their steps and begin again.

The historical difficulties started by Dr. Pusey are well known to all who have at all studied the relation of the See of Rome to the other Churches. Such anomalies, even if more than apparent, make no way against the whole current of Patristic teaching running in the other direction; but probably, if we could get at all the facts of the case, the difficulty in each instance would disappear. The case of Meletius, for example, presents a very different view from that given in the "Eirenicon," as we find it stated by Socrates, who wrote in the next century, and whose account must be familiar to Dr. Pusey.

It seems that the case of St. Meletius was one
of a disputed succession such as occurred at
different times in the line of the Roman Pontiffs,
depending chiefly on some disputed question of
fact, when Catholics and even Saints took
opposite sides. Meletius had been chosen Bishop
by the Arian majority in Antioch. After his
election he gradually declared himself Catholic,
and a large body of Arians conformed to the
Catholic faith, adhering to Meletius, while the
Arian party rejected him. Paulinus was soon
after chosen and consecrated Bishop by the old
Catholic party, who would have nothing to do
with Meletius because he had been elected by
the votes of the Arians. Rome and the West,
on such evidence as reached them, adhered to
the side of Paulinus, and did not acknowledge
Meletius. Socrates, however, informs us that a
mutual understanding was come to between the
two parties, that both Bishops should rule each
over his own congregation, and that on the death
of either the survivor should be recognised as
sole Bishop. He tells us that this put an end to
the dispute, and there was no longer any division
amongst the people.* This happened a year or
more before the Council of Constantinople, at
which Meletius presided, and during the sitting
of which he died. It is, then, hard to see on what
grounds Dr. Pusey makes the assertion that
Meletius presided at the Council and died while
out of communion with Rome, whereas Socrates
tells us that the dispute or schism was at an end
at least a year before the Council. There does
not appear to be any evidence which makes it
clear that he was ever out of communion with

* Socr. *Eccl. Hist.* v. 5.

Rome at all. On the other hand, it is certain that Meletius communicated with Bishops with whom Rome was in full communion, such as St. Basil, St. Cyril, St Gregory Nazianzen, St. Chrysostom, as well as the whole Council of Constantinople; and this could not have been, had he been considered by them, or by Rome, as out of communion, since it is notorious that to communicate with those who were out of communion was always held as *ipso facto* involving excommunication.

The next proposition sounds strangely paradoxical. "The English Church has not rejected a visible head, and is not more independent of Rome than Africa was in the time of St. Augustine."

One would be very glad to hear this, if one could see any sense in which it could be true; but where is the proof of it? Probably it will astonish most of Dr. Pusey's Anglican readers even more than it surprises us. He shows, indeed, clearly enough that St. Augustine denounced in very strong language the carrying appeals to Rome in cases which by the Canons were to be decided before local synods. "If presbyters, deacons, and other inferior Clergy (he quotes from St. Augustine) shall in any cause which they have, complain of the judgment of their own Bishops, let the neighbouring Bishops hear and determine the matter between them, being called in by them, with consent of their own Bishops. But if they think that they should appeal from these too, let them not appeal to courts beyond the seas, but either to the Primates of their Province, or to a General Council of

Africa, as has often been enacted about Bishops also. But if any one choose to appeal to the parts beyond the seas, let him be received to communion by no one in Africa."

Dr. Pusey adds, " The English Church in the 15th century acquiesced in, or consented to, the suppression of appeals to Rome. The African Church in the 5th century not only forbade them, but excommunicated any one who should so appeal." Yet Dr. Pusey would not deny that St. Augustine in his writings furnishes a link of that long chain of tradition which runs through all Patristic teaching, in regard to the prerogatives of the Apostolic See, and the Chair of Peter. St. Augustine himself, in the case of Pelagius, sends to the Pope the decrees of two African Synods, by which he had been condemned. Pope Innocent, in reply, affirms the rights of his See in the strongest language. St. Augustine in his letter on the subject writes of the Pope, "He hath answered to all as was right, and as it became the Prelate of the Apostolic See. Already the decrees of two Councils on this matter have been sent to the Apostolic See, from whence the rescripts have been received. The cause is terminated." Again, in his 43rd Epistle, he speaks of the " Roman Church in which hath always flourished the Primacy of the Apostolic Chair, Apostolicæ Cathedræ Principatus." Dr. Pusey speaks as if the question of appeals covered the whole case of the Papal claims. It is clear that St. Augustine was of a different opinion, and did not intend, while protesting against certain abuses in matters of appeal, to detract from that authority to which he himself appealed as to the highest and last tribunal in matters of doctrine ;

for certainly this seems to be the natural sense of the memorable words "Apostolicæ Cathedræ Principatus," and "inde recepta sunt rescripta, causa finita est." And surely this restraining of uncanonical appeals to Rome is a very different thing from the formal declaration required of all the Anglican Clergy, that "the Pope hath no jurisdiction in this realm of England."

Dr. Pusey quotes a devout and loyal Catholic like Gerson, speaking strong words against abuses of Papal authority; but we may be sure Gerson, who had been the great light at the Councils of Basle and Constance, would have died rather than have impugned that Primacy of jurisdiction in the See of Peter which a few years later the Council of Florence declared to be of Divine institution. Gerson's words are these, as quoted by Dr. Pusey: "A General Council, representing the Universal Church, if it aim to see complete union, to repress and put an end to schisms, and to exalt the Church, must before all things, after the manner of the Holy Fathers before us, limit and bound the co-active and usurped power of the Pope, which at successive times many supreme Pontiffs obtained to themselves, contrary to God and justice, depriving inferior Bishops of the power and authority given them by God and the Church." Nothing that Dr. Pusey brings forward is much stronger against abuse of authority by the See of Rome than the words he quotes of Pope Nicholas V., who certainly did not intend to repudiate that jurisdiction of the Holy See which is of Divine right, but only to admit that Popes being human may abuse and have abused the authority committed to them by God for edification. The words of Pope Nicholas, as given by Dr. Pusey, are: "The Roman Pontiffs, it seems to me, extended their skirts too far, in that they left no jurisdiction to the other Bishops; those of Basle abridged too much the power of the Apostolic See; but so it happens, whoso doth things unworthy must endure things unjust, those who would set erect a tree inclined on one side, draw it on the other. Our mind is, not to despoil of their rights the Bishops who are called to a part of our charge, for so we hope to preserve our own jurisdiction if we do not usurp what belongs to others." If Anglicans will accept that Primacy of jurisdiction given by our Lord to Peter, which St. Augustine recognised in his successor, and which was afterwards defined and accepted by East and West at the Council of Florence, the limits of that jurisdiction.can easily be settled, and the line drawn between what is Divine and what of ecclesiastical institution, in the actual jurisdiction of the Roman Pontiffs. The separation between England and the Church took place and is perpetuated, not merely because appeals to Rome were abolished, but because all that was of Divine and all that was of human origin, in the jurisdiction of the Pope, was rejected together, and is rejected still in the oath of supremacy; and also because essential changes, of a character no less heretical than schismatic, were introduced or accepted by the Church of England. Such, for instance, was the repudiation of the Sacrament of Extreme Unction from the Service Book, and that tampering with the Liturgy which has obscured, to say the least, if it has not absolutely excluded, the doctrine of the Eucharistic Sacrifice. To these and other such acts the Church of England stands committed, so long as she retains her present Service Book; and until such acts are repented and retracted, it seems almost idle to speak of hopes for reunion. But where so much advance has been made in the right direction, we must hope that the rest of the way will ere long be traversed.

The greater part of the remainder of the volume is taken up with proving what most Catholics would be quite ready to admit, that many exaggerated things have been said by Catholic writers of name, concerning the Pope's official infallibility, on the prerogatives of the Blessed Virgin, and on many other subjects. No doubt, viewed from without, there is some matter for perplexity in this whole subject. We know that many persons, now Catholics, have been for years kept back from seeing the Church's claims on their absolute allegiance, because of the hold these exaggerated statements had obtained on their imagination, and the repugnance they felt in themselves to the aspect of doctrine thus presented. This has arisen partly from their having attributed to such statements an authority which they did not really possess, and from their not distinguishing between matters of faith and matters of pious opinion; partly also because they did not make allowance for the exaggeration of rhetorical statements and the use of words in the second intention. Catholics, on the other hand, especially those who have been always Catholics, are not much troubled at these things. They know that the Church while requiring *unitas in necessariis* is most free in conceding *libertas in dubiis*, that there are schools of opinion in the Church, that great latitude is permitted in

the unauthoritative expression of devotional
sentiment, and that almost any amount of bad
taste is tolerated; in a word, that the Church
does not aim at creating a dead and soulless
level of uniformity, but tolerates great liberty in
matters of opinion, provided her children accept
her as their Mother and Mistress in Divine
Truth, and are always ready to submit to her
decision, should she, through her legitimate
organs, think fit to pronounce a judgment.
Thus she secures to her children the habit of
faith and obedience, and the right exercise of
their reason and free will. And so Catholics
learn from the Church a large spirit of forbearance and toleration, and put up with the views
of others which do not involve a difference of
faith, expecting a like forbearance in return.

As for exaggeration of statement, it is the
tendency of the human mind to exaggerate;
because our judgements are influenced at least
as much by the sensitive as by the intellectual
part of our being. We speak from what we feel,
quite as much as from what we know. And so,
when we have to oppose error or defend truth,
the more we feel the greatness of the truth,
the more difficult do we find it not to over-
state what we mean. Moreover, feeling the in-
adequacy of human language to express all we
feel and know, we easily fall into exaggerations, trusting to other statements, made elsewhere or on other occasions, to qualify our
expressions and prevent a misconception of our
meaning. Thus, for example, no one has made
more of the intercession of Mary than St.
Bernard, yet no one has shown more clearly
than the sainted author of the " Jesu dulcis

memoriæ," that Jesus was his all in all, or could have said more absolutely—

> Simply to His grace and wholly,
> Life and light and strength belong,
> And I love supremely, solely,
> Him the Holy, Him the strong.*

Much the same may be said in behalf of St. Alphonsus Liguori.

If Dr. Pusey were a Catholic, or were well acquainted with the practical working of the Catholic religion in the lives of pious Catholics, he might not, indeed, approve of all that was done or said amongst them, but he would acquit them of taking from our Lord any of the love they give to His Mother, and provided he accepted the statement of the Council of Trent that "the Saints reigning with Christ intercede for us, and that it is good for us to invoke them," he would find himself left pretty free as to the devotional expression of this belief.

But it is a wonderful advance on the usual forms of Protestant Controversy, when we find these subjects treated, not with the exaggeration of the vulgar controversialist, but with the calmness and precision of the theologian, however much his position outside the Church may necessarily distort his view, as a painting can never be seen properly except from the right point of sight. It is a great consolation, and opens a new phase of the controversy, to find a writer in the position of Dr. Pusey, after expressing himself most strongly against what he calls exaggerations in "the practical Roman system," concluding that "the breach with Rome has been

* Newman's *Gerontius.*

widened unduly," and again that "Rome need not make such things terms of communion, nor need she insist that the Church of England, if united with her, should receive them, but provision might be made formally, on both sides, that she need not."

Again, "I doubt not that the Roman Church and ourselves are kept apart much more by that vast practical system which lies beyond the letter of the Council of Trent, things which are taught with a *quasi* authority in the Roman Church, than by what is actually defined." He then goes on, strangely enough, to draw a distinction between those who are born Roman Catholics, "who have a liberty," and converts, who, he says, "in the nature of things, cannot have the liberty, of choosing what opinions and practices to adopt on open questions," and adds: "For myself, I have always felt that had the English Church, by accepting heresy, driven me out, I could have gone in no other way than that of closing my eyes and accepting whatever was put before me; but a liberty which individuals could not use, and explanations which, so long as they remained individual, must be unauthoritative, might be formally made by the Church of Rome to the Church of England, as the basis of reunion." Further on he says: "If Englishmen speak against Papal authority it is not in itself (which would be a matter of indifference), but as an authority which, if they submitted to it, would enforce upon them that practical system. Probably, too, there is an hereditary dread of the renewal of the fires of Smithfield, the sinfulness of which has never been disowned." Speaking of his hopes for the unity of Christendom, he says:

"Years ago we seemed to be in the position of the Heaven-controlled seer: 'I see him, but not nigh; I behold him, but not now.' And meanwhile our office was within ourselves; we could not propose union, while we ourselves were so disunited. I hoped that the passing storm of unbelief, which I have seen in the distance these forty years, would drive together those who loved Jesus. I hoped that as we became united in the truth, and in the characteristic principles of our Church, those other great portions of the Church, East and West, would see that God is in us of a truth. Why should not the Church again be united in that faith which she held before a miserable quarrel first caused disunion? . . . . Apart from other evils, the strength is wasted against each other, which should be concentrated against the common foe of Jesus, and of all who are His. The organic reunion of Christendom, and of the Protestant bodies too, has been held to be possible even by the Ultramontanes in the Roman Church. Cardinal Wiseman quoted, nearly a quarter of a century ago, the expressions of 'the profound and pious Mohler.' 'After observing,' he says, 'that no Catholic can refuse to acknowledge with humiliation the corruptions of past ages, that the proof of this lies in the very existence of Protestantism, which could not have existed without them,' he thus concludes: 'Behold the ground on which the two Churches will one day meet and clasp hands. In the consciousness of our common fault let us cry out to one another, one and all, "We have all erred; the Church alone could not fail. We have all sinned; the Church alone is pure from stain."'"
Again, Dr. Pusey quotes the words of the Count

de Maistre. The extract is from Gladstone's Remarks on the Royal Supremacy, and this Catholic writer is quoted by him as belonging to "the strictest sect of the Ultramontane school." "If ever Christians are to be brought together, as everything invites them, it seems that the movement should take its beginning from the Church of England . . . . the Church of England, which touches us with one hand, touches with the other those whom we cannot touch. And though in a certain point of view . . . . it presents the ridiculous spectacle of a rebel preaching obedience, yet in another aspect, it is *most precious*, and may be considered, like some chemical medium, capable of uniting together elements which, of their own nature, cannot amalgamate." "It is now sixty years," Mr. Gladstone continues, in the extract given by Dr. Pusey, "since thus a stranger and an alien, a stickler to the extremest point for the prerogatives of his Church, and nursed in every prepossession against us, turning his eye across the channel, although he could then only see the English Church in the lethargy of her organization and the dull twilight of her learning, could nevertheless discern that there was a very special work written of God for her in Heaven, and that she was VERY PRECIOUS to the Christian world. O, how serious a rebuke to those who, not strangers but suckled at her breast, . . . have written concerning her even as men might write that were hired to make a case against her, and by an adverse instinct in the selection of evidence, and a severity of construction such as no history of the deeds of man can bear, have often in these last years put her to an open shame."

Dr. Pusey refers to the Association for the
Unity of Christendom with great hopefulness.
"And now," he says, "God seems again to be
awakening the yearning to be visibly one, and
He who alone, the Author of Peace and Lover
of Concord, must have put it into men's minds
to pray for the unity of Christendom, will in His
time, we trust, fulfil the prayer which He Himself
has taught."

Dr. Pusey's conclusion is a strong protest
against what he terms "the present theory of
Papal infallibility." "The Ultramontanes in the
Roman Communion seem to be drifting off
further from the principles of the early and
undivided Church. . . . The shores of Italy seem
ever to be receding. . . . In the Gallican Church
a century and a half ago there seemed to be a
dawn of reunion. Now things seem to be taking
an opposite direction." He concludes by saying
that to those who would hold the opinions of
Bossuet, he and those who would act with him,
"stretch forth their hands." The strife with
unbelief stretches and strains the powers of the
Church everywhere; Satan's armies are united,
at least, in their warfare against the truth as it
is in Jesus. Are those who would maintain the
faith in Him alone to be at variance? On the
terms which Bossuet, we hope, would have
sanctioned, we long to see the Church united;
to all who in East or West desire to see intercommunion restored among those who hold the
faith of the undivided Church, we say, This is
not our longing only; this is impressed on our
Liturgy by those who were before us; for this,
whenever we celebrate the Holy Eucharist, we
are bound to pray that God would inspire

continually the Universal Church with the spirit of truth, unity, and concord. For this I pray daily. For this I would gladly die. O Lord, tarry not."

Such is the conclusion of this remarkable book. It has been my endeavour to let the author, as far as possible, speak for himself: to present his mind to my readers; not to refute, still less to accept his arguments. The book certainly requires an answer; but I cannot help my strong impression, that the best answer to it will come one day from Dr. Pusey himself. I mean, of course, in as far as it impugns any Catholic dogma—for on all the rest Dr. Pusey might retain his opinions, if he and those who think with him were members of the Roman obedience. A great aid towards this consummation would be a disposition on our side to explain, and to receive explanations, in a conciliatory spirit. The book unquestionably is a most clearly pronounced endeavour to find a basis for reunion, on the principles debated between Archbishop Wake and the Gallican divines two centuries ago.* And here two questions arise. First, how far is Dr. Pusey authorised to speak in the name of the Church of England, or backed by any large body of the clergy and laity, headed by any minority however small of the Bishops? The second question is, how far the authorities of the Catholic Church

* It has been suggested in some quarters that Wake's real object was to detach the French Church from communion with Rome. Such is certainly not the sense of Dr. Pusey's reference to him, for when Archdeacon Wordsworth propounded that view in the *Guardian* he at once wrote to contradict it.

would be ready at this day to accept such advances if they were really made? To the first of these questions this is not the place to offer an answer. The only satisfactory reply must soon appear, in the mode in which the book is received in the Church of England. To the second I would desire to reply with great diffidence. But it is not going beyond what we have been accustomed to read in approved theologians, and to receive from the lips and pen of our own Bishops, if we answer, that such advances, if made by any large bodies of separatists, would be met by our authorities in a conciliatory spirit;* and that, for the healing of a schism, any lawful concessions would be gladly made. Even those who most strongly hold that what are commonly called the Ultra-montane opinions are the more logical, the legitimate deduction from Scripture, the true development of Patristic teaching, and who would prefer a union of all Christians on this basis, would nevertheless hold most strongly that *reunion on the principles of Bossuet would be better than perpetuated schism.* Whether such negotiations may ever actually take place, or how it may please God to direct the issue, no man can pretend to foresee. It *may* not be God's way of mercy for England, but we may not dare to say that it *cannot* be. Meanwhile, we may well look hopefully on any movement tending in that direction. To all Anglicans who hold with Dr. Pusey, and would that we had reason to think that he represents the great body of his Church, we would say from our hearts—God speed. And because the mighty changes in

---

* Cardinal Wiseman's *Letter to Lord Shrewsbury.*

H

minds and wills that must take place before such a consummation can be possible, must be simply the effect of grace, and the fruit of prayer, therefore placing our whole confidence in sincere and united prayer, must we hail it as the most hopeful sign of all, that Anglicans are themselves praying for unity. To the members of their Association of prayer for the Unity of Christendom we address ourselves, inviting them to join with us in the petition, that all the Baptized may be brought within the Fold of Visible Unity under the Successor of Peter, whom Christ the Good Shepherd hath set over His whole Flock. It is this which we mean when we pray for the Unity of Christendom. This is the object of the constant prayer of every devout Catholic; he may ask for it specifically, as a member of some special organisation for this purpose; and no doubt it would be a great encouragement to sustained and united prayer if we should see established amongst us, with the sanction of authority, an Association of prayer for the reunion of all the Baptized within the Visible Fold of Christ. Such Associations have indeed from time to time been set upon by zealous and fervent servants of God, like the late Father Ignatius Spencer and others, but we fear they have too generally languished after a time, and need now to be resuscitated by an apostolic zeal directed by authority. But, without any such organisation, the prayer for unity goes up continually to the throne of God; it is implied each time that we say " Thy Kingdom come " in the " Our Father," and is prayed for expressly by each Priest when standing daily before the Altar he recites the prayer before Communion for the

Peace and Unity of the One and Indivisible Church of God.

While admitting that it is fairly open to Catholic readers to form a different estimate of Dr. Pusey's already celebrated "Eirenicon," I have distinctly indicated that my own view is favourable to it, as a whole, understanding its main drift to be a seeking after unity, and not after pretexts for division. It has, in fact, appeared to me the most unequivocal advance in that direction made since the Reformation, being a clearly pronounced endeavour to find a basis for reunion in what are commonly known as the principles of the Gallican Divines. This estimate of the work receives a strong confirmation from Dr. Pusey's Letter to the *Weekly Register* of November 25, 1865. If it be true that an honest man is the best interpreter of his own meaning— and few will deny that Dr. Pusey is an *honest* man—then it is clear that I have not misconceived the true sense of the "Eirenicon." He writes, "I thank you with all my heart for your kind-hearted and appreciative review of my 'Eirenicon.' I am thankful that you have brought out the main drift and object of it, *that which, in my mind, underlies the whole*, to show that, in my conviction, there is no insurmountable obstacle to the union of the Roman, Greek, and Anglican communions. I have long been convinced that *there is nothing in the Council of Trent which could not be explained satisfactorily to us* if it were explained *authoritatively*, i.e., by the Roman Church herself, not by individual theologians only;" and again, "I thank you for that tenderness which enabled you to see my aim and objects throughout a long and necessarily miscellaneous work." He then goes on to say that whatever there was controversial in his book he had said only on "the defensive, not as a reformer;" and again, "I do not presume to prescribe to Italians or Spaniards what they shall hold, or how they shall express their *pious opinions*, and least of all did I think of imputing to any of the writers whom I quoted" (such as St. Bernard, St. Alphonsus Liguori, Faber, and others) "that they took from our Lord any of the love which they gave to His Mother. I was intent only on describing the system which I believe is the great obstacle to reunion. I had not the least thought of criticising holy men who held it."

On the subject of the prerogatives of the Sovereign Pontiff, Dr. Pusey expresses, not indeed the Catholic doctrine, but puts forth as his own an opinion so much beyond what we have been accustomed to hear even from advanced Anglicans, that we feel sure it will be read by most Catholics with unmixed surprise and satisfaction. "I have not intended," he says, "to express any opinion about a visible head of the Church. We readily recognise the Primacy of the Bishop of Rome; the bearings of that Primacy upon other local Churches we believe to be matter of ecclesiastical, not of Divine law. But neither is there. anything in the Supremacy, in itself, to which we should object."

In another part of his letter he writes, "I believe that the hopes which you have held out that the authorities of the Roman Communion might hold, 'that reunion on the principles of Bossuet would be better than perpetuated schism,' will unlock many a pent-up longing,

pent-up on the ground of its apparent hopelessness." The concluding words of this beautiful
and consoling letter are: "If hope is revived in
the English mind that Christendom may again
be united, rekindled hope will ascend in more
fervent prayer to Him 'who maketh men to be
of one mind in an house,' and our prayers will
not return unheard for want of love."

It was clearly therefore no mistake to say that
Dr. Pusey's principal object was to ascertain
whether a reunion of Anglicans with the Catholic Church be possible on what are commonly
called Gallican principles, and that he accepts
the suggestion I had ventured to throw out, that
a reunion on the principles of Bossuet would be
better than perpetuated schism. The gist of the
whole work, then, may be fairly reduced to this
single issue, and so I intend to treat it. It is
right in doing so to enter somewhat more deeply
into the matter in its practical bearings, and to
look in the face some of the principal difficulties
which meet us at the outset, and state candidly
what may be thought of them. I would speak
of course with great diffidence, feeling moreover
that it is an ungracious thing to suggest difficulties, and yet that it would not be acting
loyally by Anglicans to ignore their existence.
To speak only of the hopes, and say nothing of
the difficulties of reunion, would be like inviting
people to an aerial tour through the tranquil
heavens, with charming prospects of earth and
sea and sky above and around, without warning
them that the course of the wind might at any
moment bring them up short against the Peak of
Teneriffe. I do not say, since "all things are
possible to God," that such difficulties are in-

superable, only that they must be steadily looked
in the face.

I. In the first place, then, what are actually
the principles of Bossuet, taking him as a fair
sample, theologically, of the Gallican school?
For these we have not far to go, for they are
stated very concisely in Bossuet's well-known
work entitled, "Exposition de la Doctrine de
l'Eglise Catholique," and it may be well to
premise, that probably few books have ever
received a greater number of approbations, from
Bishops, Cardinals, Roman congregations, and
from the Pope himself.

Thirty pages of the volume are taken up with
these approbations only, including two briefs of
Pope Innocent the Eleventh addressed to the
author. In these the Pope says: "We judge the
work not only worthy to be praised and approved
by us, but also to be read and esteemed by all
the world. We hope that this work, by the
grace of God, will produce much fruit. We trust
that it will be found useful and may aid in pro-
pagating the orthodox faith." In the second
Brief it is called "a wise and pious exposition of
the Catholic Faith, and an admirable work."
This will suffice to commend Bossuet's Exposition of the Faith to the attention of Anglican
readers, as an authorised exposition of Catholic
doctrine: most educated Catholics are of course
acquainted with the work. Passing over the
chapters on the worship of God, the invocation
of Saints, the religious uses of images and relics,
on justification and the merits of good works,
purgatory and indulgences, the Real Presence
and the Sacrifice of the Mass, let us come to the
chapters treating of the Church and its Head.

After having spoken of the Holy Ghost, the
Spirit of Truth, the author goes on in the next
paragraph to speak in order of the Church, the
visible and perpetual organ and mouth-piece or
oracle of the same Holy Spirit. " It is thus," he
says, " that the children of God acquiesce in the
judgment of the Church, believing that they
receive from its mouth the oracle of the Holy
Spirit; therefore it is that after we have said in
the Creed, 'I believe in the Holy Ghost,' we
add immediately, 'the Holy Catholic Church,'
whereby we bind ourselves to recognise one
truth infallible and perpetual in the Universal
Church, since that Church, which we believe has
existed in all ages, would have ceased to be the
Church if it had ceased to teach the revealed
truth of God." The last chapter of the work is
on " The Authority of the Holy See and of the
Episcopate." " As the Son of God willed that
His Church should be one, and solidly founded
on unity, He established and instituted the
Primacy of St. Peter in order to maintain and
cement this unity. Wherefore we recognise this
very Primacy in the successors of the Prince of
the Apostles, to whom, for this reason, we owe
that submission and obedience which the Holy
Councils and the Holy Fathers have always en-
joined on the faithful.

" As to those points which are known to be
disputed by the schools, although often quoted
by the reformed ministers, in order to cast odium
on the authority of the Holy See, it is unneces-
sary to allude to them here, as they are not of
the Catholic faith. It is sufficient to recognise a
Head established by God to conduct the whole
Flock in His ways; to this all those who love

fraternal concord and ecclesiastical unanimity will readily agree.

"Certainly if the authors of the pretended Reformation had loved unity, they would not have abolished the episcopal government, which was established by Jesus Christ Himself, and was in full force in the apostolic age, nor would they have despised the authority of St. Peter's Chair, which has such a sure foundation in the Gospel, and so manifest a sequel in tradition, but rather, they would have carefully preserved the authority of the Episcopate, which maintains unity in particular Churches, and the Primacy of St. Peter's Chair, which is the common centre of Catholic unity."

Such is a short exposition of the principles of Bossuet, concerning the Visible Church, which is further developed in the larger works of theologians like De la Hogue, or in the most recent works of Bouvier and others of the same school. The Gallicans held the perpetual visibility and infallibility of the Church, that it was One, Holy, Catholic, Apostolic, and also Roman, because it was a visible, living body, through an essential union with a visible Head, and they taught that the Bishop of Rome was, as successor of Peter, the divinely-appointed Head of the Church, its centre and mouthpiece, apart from whom the Church was not. All this they taught, basing their doctrine on the decrees of the Councils of Florence and of Trent concerning the Supreme Pontiff and his prerogatives in the Church of Christ. Now, are Anglicans prepared to accept this doctrine concerning the Visible Church and its Head? Dr. Pusey, in the name of his school, has already answered in the affirmative, though the statement of these doctrines in his book, and even in his letter, falls short of an acceptance of Bossuet's doctrine. If, however, this is his meaning, the ground has already been laid down authoritatively, and the judgment of the Holy See expressed in a Pontifical Brief, in favour of the soundness of the principles of Bossuet on the Visible Church and its Head with sufficient clearness to serve as the basis of reunion for any number of individuals, or of Churches.

II. But here comes in the chief difficulty, if, as I fear, there are very few even of advanced Anglicans who would define the Visible Church and its Head with Dr. Pusey, supposing him to accept unreservedly the principles of Bossuet, which does not seem certain. For the Church cannot recede a single step from the teaching already laid down in the Council of Trent, concerning the Visible Church and its Head; and the Council of Trent did not, on this point, go beyond what had been already decreed by East and West at the Council of Florence. The words of that Council are as follows:—"Moreover we define that the Holy Apostolic See and the Bishop of Rome is successor to the Blessed Peter, Chief of the Apostles, true Vicar of Christ, Head of the whole Church, and Father and Teacher of all Christians; that to him was given in the person of Blessed Peter the full power to conduct, to rule, and to govern the whole Catholic Church, according to that mode which is determined in the Acts of Œcumenical Councils, and the Holy Canons." It is clear, therefore, that there is no way of conciliating what is commonly called the *branch theory* of the Visible Church with the definitions of Florence and of Trent, or with the opinions of Bossuet and the Gallican school, which were based on these definitions; and hence, on Gallican principles, the Anglicans have been all along outside the Visible Church. But is there then no possible basis of negotiation for reunion, without a full previous admission on the part of separated bodies that they are out of the Visible Church? The true reply is, that the history of the Council of Florence furnishes an analogy applicable, at least in great part, to the case of the Anglicans. This appears from the learned work on the Oriental Church by Pitzipios, printed in Rome ten years ago at the Propaganda Press. Whatever may be the doctrine of the Greeks at the present day concerning the Visible Church, it seems clear that at the time of the Council of Florence they must have held some such theory as Anglicans now hold; yet we nowhere find that they are required, either before or after the act of union, to admit that they had been in *formal schism*. The only way of accounting for the mode in which the Oriental Bishops were treated at Ferrara and Florence, is by supposing that the authorities of the Catholic Church laid down and acted on a broad distinction between *material* and *formal* schism. The Patriarch of Constantinople and his train of Bishops, though they were considered by the Pope as actual schismatics, were not treated as rebels. In the great Church of St. George at Ferrara, seats of honour were placed for the Pope and the Western Bishops on the left side of the High Altar, while a similar position to the right of the High Altar was assigned to the Patriarch of Constantinople and the Oriental Bishops, thrones being placed on either side for the Emperor of Germany, who was absent, and the Emperor of Constantinople, while in the midst, on a magnificent throne in front of the Altar, was exposed the Book of the Holy Gospels. The Pope opened the Sacred Synod by intoning the *Benedictus*, "Blessed be the Lord God of Israel, for He hath visited and Redeemed His people," and all joined together in psalms and canticles. Then was read from the Ambon the invitation to the Council and excommunication of all who should not assent to its decrees; first on the part of the Patriarch of Constantinople and afterwards on that of the Pope, declaring the convocation and opening of the Council. This distinction between material and formal schism may also account for the fact, that the Greeks were not required to repudiate the Saints of their Communion, who had been canonized during the Schism. In the same way in the great Western Schism of the Anti-Popes, there were Saints of both obediences and yet it is certain that there was only one true Pope, and therefore the adherents of one side or the other were at least in material schism. Of course, the case of the Anti-Popes is only an analogy, as far as it goes; and so also is the case of the Council of Florence. Neither can be said to cover the case of the Anglicans, if for no other reason, because the orders of the Oriental Church were universally recognised; while those of Anglicans, up to this moment, have never been admitted amongst ourselves. Nevertheless it is clear that the mode in which the Oriental Bishops were treated was not simply owing to the respect due to their orders, which would not make them a whit less schismatical, but was based on the broad and solid distinction between material and formal schism. And this principle would hold good with certain differences, if any body of baptized Christians, such as the Lutherans of Germany, or the Presbyterians of Scotland, should make advances for negotiations with the Catholic Church, with a view to admission into visible unity. For argument's sake, and to prevent any confusion of the real question with that of Anglican orders (on which I do not intend to enter), let us consider the case of Anglicans in respect of material or formal schism on no higher grounds, and try to judge of their relation to the Church and the relation of the Church to them from this point only; as if, for instance, it were the case of the Lutherans formerly, debated between Bossuet and Leibnitz. We are still brought to the conclusion that admission of fundamental error need not necessarily be required of separated bodies, as a previous condition of negotiations for reunion or submission.

III. But suppose that not only Dr. Pusey, but a large body who are willing to be represented by him, are prepared for *bonâ fide* negotiations for reunion on the principles of Bossuet, and that the authorities of the Catholic Church have formally accepted negotiations on this basis; here occurs a difficulty, so great as to be almost overwhelming. Dr. Pusey represents, as yet, only a school of opinion. Not one English Bishop has publicly identified himself with this school, and few of the Anglican Bishops ever lose an opportunity of publishing their energetic dissent from many of the doctrines which he and those who think with him hold as integral portions of the Faith. Let me refer to a remarkable Anglican sermon which states this same difficulty far better than I can, whilst it offers some solution of it.* The author quotes from the *Christian Remembrancer:* " Within the English Church there exists a large school, who look upon the desire to unite with Rome in any form as sinful, and who must *pari passu* be conciliated, unless the unity of Christendom is to determine the break-up of the Church of England." The writer of the sermom comments thus on the words quoted : " We have no desire to make light of this very serious consideration, and no honest discussion of our present subject can escape its force and urgency. There are, it may be, some among us who would make short work with it. They would regard expulsion of the so-termed Evangelicals from the Church as a blessing only inferior to the reunion of Catholic-minded Churchmen with the Latin and Greek communions. We cannot agree with them in this judgment. . . . . But no one who is really acquainted with the actual tone and working of the Church of England can deny that the ' Evangelical ' clergy, on the whole, are steadily advancing towards a higher measure of truth than they had attained in past years. ' Evangelicalism,' indeed, is as the womb of Rebecca : it contains a Jacob and an Esau. To some souls its attraction lies in the fact that it rationalistically ignores or denies Sacramental Truth. To others, a fundamentally different class of minds, its charm consists in that love of, and

* Sermon by the late Canon Liddon in Second Series of *Sermons on Reunion of Christendom.* London : Hayes.

devotion to, the Person of our Blessed Redeemer
which has undeniably characterised its general
history. And as those who are attracted by its
negative aspects are continually sinking, and
become, as opportunity arises, the easy prey of
Rationalism; so those who are drawn by its
positive Faith and Love are, under the guidance
of the Blessed Spirit, as perpetually rising, and
they furnish its best recruits to the cause of
Catholicism. Indeed, the advance of Rationalism, fraught as it is with the utmost danger to
the salvation of many precious souls, does in-
cidentally help to reduce, as in the long run it
may probably destroy altogether, the difficulty
before us. It acts as a solvent upon the popular
Evangelicalism. It precipitates the anti-sac-
ramental negative element towards the pure
Rationalism with which, under the common
name of Free Thought, it has the strongest and
most radical affinities. It drives the adoring and
believing element upwards, to take shelter from its
devastating and its unspiritual action in a sincere
allegiance to the principle of Church authority.
This disintegration of Evangelicalism is going
on rapidly beneath our eyes, and every attack
upon the books of Holy Scripture, nay more,
every serious inquiry into the historical origin
and authority of the Sacred Canon, is a certain,
although unnoticed, step in its gradual progress.
And we rejoice to believe that while, alas, only
too many in that great party are day by day
forfeiting, at the bidding of Rationalistic principles, the light and warmth which has hereto-
fore streamed upon their souls from the Sun of
Righteousness, the great majority are truer to
the loftier instincts of their spiritual nature than

to the logical exigencies of their theory, and are moving, amid whatever defections and relapses, towards the full acceptance of the Faith.

"If this be so, we may trust that in the kindly Providence of our gracious Lord the restored unity of Chistendom, if it be granted to us, will not determine in the break-up of the Church of England. It may coincide, in point of time, with the final retirement from our communion of those who bend in reality before no Truth whatever, as revealed and certain; and to whom the language of the Prayer Book, from the daily Morning Absolution down to the Visitation of the Sick, is, when they steadily reflect upon its import, a standing cause of offence. But among these, too, there are generous souls; and God may have for them and for us a future in store of which we cannot yet discern the bearings. Enough, at any rate, has been said to show that, short of active conciliation of the 'Evangelical' party—a most sacred duty, be it remarked, so far as loyalty to truth permits—there are causes at work which may re-assure us, when we consider the very formidable objection to any practical scheme for reunion among Catholic Chrisians of the Greek, and Roman, and Anglican Churches, the objection which is based on the position and numbers of the 'Evangelical' party in the latter communion." Having spoken of the causes which he sees in operation amongst the various sections of his own Church, in which he thinks he discerns afar off the principles of unity and truth working themselves to order out of chaos, he speaks also of the relations in which his Church stands "to the great Churches of Christendom." "It would be at once disingenuous and unpractical to ignore the fact that the 'secondary matters' which divide the greater Churches of Christendom are of graver import than any question of Liturgical form.

"More points of difference might be named—some of them serious ones. But our present purpose is not to enumerate, still less to exaggerate them. It is our duty to recognise them. There they are, patent and painful facts; nor will any scheme of reunion have a chance of success which postulates simple submission from one side, and claims Œcumenicity for the other. The questions which divide the Churches must be regarded, *pro tanto*, as open questions; 'open,' that is, not absolutely, but to the revision of an Œcumenical Council, when such may be had. And if any should say or think that to anticipate the assembling of such a representation of Christendom in our own day is a visionary imagination; or that, if assembled, it could ever introduce the reign of harmony into the realms of ecclesiastical discord, let us reflect that God has taught His people their deepest lessons by the pressure of suffering inflicted from without. None can mark the upgrowth and power of the infidel spirit in Europe without seeing that we are drifting rapidly towards a time more like that of the first three centuries of the Church's life than any subsequent period has been. The religion of Jesus Christ has experienced in turn all the relations towards the worldly power which are abstractedly possible. It has survived persecution; it has survived, more marvellously still, ages of wealth and power; it has lived on under a cold neutrality; and it might seem as if the cycle thus completed might, ere long, begin over again. In the infidel literature of Europe, there are ominous threats and undisguised passions, which remind us that the spirit which cried of old, 'Christianos ad leones,' is not extinct. That spirit will re-appear in England with those fuller developments of Rationalism, which are apparently inevitable, and we may hope that suffering in a common cause, if such be the will of our Divine Lord, will teach those who should be brothers to understand each other. Meanwhile, existing differences may be lawfully minimized; and, even if we do not see our way in the tangled maze towards a practical solution of the difficulties which they undeniably present, we may cultivate a habit of hopeful, peaceful, trustful expectancy, relying firmly on the revealed will of our Divine Lord, and looking forward to the time 'when Ephraim shall not envy Judah, and Judah shall not vex Ephraim.' To recognise difficulties is one thing, to despair of overcoming them is another."

None will fail to observe the grasp of his subject and the masterly treatment of the difficulty by this writer, nor does it need the initial letter of his name to indicate to us perhaps the most leading mind and greatest preacher that Oxford has produced since the days of Dr. Newman, and one who is likely to do more than any other man towards forming the mind of the University in its younger members.

IV. And here it seems natural to refer to another great difficulty which may be said to underlie the question of individual responsibility, and of individual submission. It is obvious that "the disintegration of the Low Church section of Anglicans," spoken of by the author of the Ser-

mon just quoted, can only be the work of time;
difficulties and delays may obstruct the project
of a General Council, to whose decision the
various sections of Anglicans might agree to
submit their differences with one another, and
their differences with the Catholic Church.
Meantime, the national Church, as a body, can
make no advances which could be accepted by
the Catholic Authorities, or even by the Oriental
or Russian Communions, because it can have no
authoritative voice, or common principle, or moral
personalty; there would be no one to treat or to
be treated with. It must continue a heteroge-
neous body, so long as it does not put from it
one of the two great schools which have always
held divided sway. How then, meantime, will
the Catholic School in the Anglican Church,
supposing it to be able legally to hold its ground,
be able to do so conscientiously, should its
members have advanced so far individually as
to be ready to seek for corporate reunion on the
principles of Bossuet and the Gallican divines?
Those divines admit, with the Council of
Florence, a dogma on the nature of the visible
Church which cannot be reconciled with the
Anglican *branch* theory. This theory therefore
and that dogma cannot stand together; and
obvious as is the distinction between material
and formal schism, yet it is no less obvious that
material schism becomes formal, when consciousness of the fact of schism begins. Human events
may defer indefinitely projects of corporate
reunion, but truth, when we know it, rests on us
with an eternal obligation, independent of all
conceivable circumstances and events. *Fiat
justitia, ruat cœlum.* If then the truth be once

made clear to us, what voice upon earth can dare to say, " Stay and work for unity," when the voice of illuminated conscience says, " Go and follow out the exigence of truth?" It was on this principle that Newman and Manning quitted years ago a vantage ground, which no one has since occupied. Far be it from us to judge any man. Each several soul before his own Master standeth or falleth. And, as regards the case of individuals, we never know where to set limits to the possibility of invincible ignorance and material schism; still it would not be right to have concluded, without guarding against the possibility of leaving a single soul to suppose that anything could justify the sacrifice of the *justum* to the *utile*, of *truth* to *expediency*, even though that expediency might seem to be to "the greater glory of God." We know not whether this present Catholic movement in the Anglican Church may have any immediate issue other than that of the former movement twenty years ago. Yet we may all pray heartily that its ultimate result may be a great corporate reunion of the National Church with the ancient Mother and Mistress of all the Churches. Or if this be not in the designs of God—and perhaps we are all too weak in faith, in charity, and in prayer to obtain so great a grace—we cannot doubt that it will issue in important results; perhaps, at first, like the former movement, only in the submission as individuals of many precious souls; perhaps in something of which we seem to discover not a few indications, a movement of all that is truest and noblest in Anglicanism in the direction of a *Free Church*, independent of State control. Should this turn out to be the more

immediate issue, such an event might be hailed
as the sure precursor of a very speedy act on the
part of such seceding body, of corporate submission to the Divine authority of the Visible
Church and of Christ's Vicar upon earth. If
Anglicanism were liberated from State control,
the Catholic element being set free would fly as
it were of its own nature to the Centre of Unity.

Then, if ever, would be the time when a large
seceding body, such as might not unfitly be
termed a free Church of England, might be in a
position to make such propositions on submission
to the Catholic Church as its members might
agree upon and deem expedient. We can
conceive that it might ask, and the Roman
authorities might grant, various explanations on
points of doctrine, or concessions on points of
discipline, if it could be shown that by so doing
some of those difficulties might be removed or
lessened which are presented by the aspect of
the Catholic religion, viewed from without, to
a nation which, like the English, has been
separated by a chasm of three centuries from
the traditions of Catholic Christendom. And so
perhaps the way might be made more plain for
the return of England, as a nation, to the Ancient
Faith.

But if, as is quite possible, neither of these
great movements should take place in our day,
though we need not at present contemplate such
an alternative, may our Lord continue the good
work which He has begun, in His own time, and
in His own way; and may we cultivate amongst
ourselves, and towards those without, a great
spirit of charity and forbearance—that charity
which hopeth all things—that so all our prayers

and good works may ascend "like incense before God," in never-ceasing intercession for the peace and unity of our Jerusalem, for the conversion of pagans, infidels, and sinners, and for the re-union* of all the Baptized who have once been made members of the Mystical Body of Christ to the visible communion of the world-wide Catholic Church!

* The following passages encourage the hope that we may before long see inaugurated by the Catholic Bishops, or with their sanction, a great " Association of prayer for the Unity of Christendom," which, it would seem, the Bishop of Mayence would energetically invite all those who believe in Christ to join. He writes: " How different is the present aspect of Christendom from that Jesus Christ prayed for, 'that they may be one, even as We are One.' It is our duty to strive to the very utmost to restore this union. No Catholic, however small his power, should refuse his help. The humblest materials are employed in the greatest buildings. But there are two chief means which, in my opinion, we can all use. The first is to pray for the reunion of all Christian confessions. Would that this unanimous prayer could be organised on a common plan, accepted by all Christian souls who long for the reunion of the various religious societies! . . . What would still more rejoice us would be to see men of different Christian communions deliberate together for organising the recital of some common prayer by all who believe that Jesus Christ is the true and only Son of God. I cannot think that God could refuse to hear such a prayer, that we should form but one body, *ut omnes unum sint.*"—From the work by Dr. Ketteler, Bishop of Mayence, entitled *Liberté, Autorité, Eglise,* p. 227.

APPENDIX.

SIR,—I beg leave to call your attention to a passage in your admirable Review last week of Dr. Pusey's recent work. It is there asserted by implication that "the statement that the Church of England is, in God's hands, the great bulwark against infidelity in this land," was "originally enunciated by Dr. Newman."

I have written in my lifetime a great deal more than I can remember, but I neither know where I have made this particular statement, nor can I conceive I ever made it, whether in print, in private letter, or in conversation. And I am sure I should not have made it deliberately. Certainly, it does not express ~~any~~ real judgment concerning the Church of England. Nor have I any reason to think that Dr. Pusey ascribes it to me.

What I said in my *Apologia* was this: "Doubtless the National Church has hitherto been a serviceable break-water against doctrinal errors more fundamental than its own."

The words "serviceable" and "breakwater" both convey the idea of something accidental and *de facto;* whereas a bulwark is an essential part of the thing defended. Moreover, in saying 'against doctrinal errors more fundamental than its own,' I simply meant that, while it happens to serve Catholic truth in one respect, nevertheless in another it has doctrinal errors, and those fundamental.

I am, Sir, your obedient servant,

JOHN H. NEWMAN.

The Oratory, Birmingham: Nov. 19, 1865.

Letter of Dr. Pusey to the " Weekly Register."

SIR,—I thank you with all my heart for your kind-hearted and appreciative view of my "Eirenicon." I am thankful that you have brought out the main drift and object of it, what, in my mind, underlies the whole, to show that, in my conviction, there is no insurmountable obstacle to the union of (you will forgive the terms, though you must reject them) the Roman, Greek, and Anglican communions. I have long been convinced that there is nothing in the Council of Trent which could not be explained *authoritatively*, i.e., by the Roman Church itself, not by individual theologians only. This involves the conviction on my side, that there is nothing in our Articles which cannot be explained rightly, as not contradicting anything held to be *de fide* in the Roman Church. The great body of the faith is held alike by both; on those subjects referred to in our Art. XXII., I believe (to use the language of a very eminent Italian nobleman) "your [our] *maximum* and our [your] *minimum* might be found to harmonise."

In regard to details of explanation, it was not
my office, as being a Priest only, invested with
no authority, to draw them out. But I wished
to indicate their possibility. You are relatively
under the same circumstances. But I believe
that the hope which you have held out, that the
authorities in the Roman communion *might* hold
" a reunion on the principles of Bossuet, would
be better than a perpetuated schism," will unlock
many a pent-up longing, pent-up on the ground
of apparent hopelessness, that Rome would
accord to the English Church any terms which it
could accept.

May I add, that nothing was further from
my wish than to write anything which should
be painful to those in your Communion? A
defence, indeed, of necessity involves some
blame; since, in a quarrel, the blame must be
wholly on the one side or on the other, or
divided; and a defence implies that it is not
wholly on the side defended. But having
smoothed down, as I believe, honestly, every
difficulty I could, to my own people, I thought
that it would not be right towards them not to
state where I conceive the real difficulty to lie.
Nor could your authorities meet our difficulties,
unless they knew them. You will think it
superfluous that I desired that none of this
system, which is now matter of " pious opinion,"
should, like the doctrine of the Immaculate
Conception, be made *de fide*. But in the view of
a hoped-for reunion, everything which you do
affects us. Let me say, too, that I did not write
as a reformer, but on the defensive. It is not
for us to prescribe to Italians or Spaniards
what they shall hold, or how they shall express

their pious opinions. All which we wish is to have it made certain by authority, that we should not, in case of reunion, be obliged to hold them ourselves. Least of all did I think of imputing to any of the writers, whom I quoted, that they "took from our Lord any of the love which they gave to His Mother." I was intent only on describing the system which I believe is the great obstacle to reunion. I had not the least thought of criticising holy men who held it.

As it is of moment that I should not be misunderstood by my own people, let me add, that I have not intended to express any opinion about a visible head of the Church. We readily recognise the Primacy of the Bishop of Rome; the bearings of that Primacy upon other local Churches we believe to be matter of ecclesiastical, not of Divine law; but neither is there anything in the Supremacy in itself to which we should object. Our only fear is, that it should, through the appointment of our Bishops, involve the reception of that practical *quasi*-authoritative system, which is, I believe, alike the cause, and (forgive me) the justification in our eyes of our remaining apart.

But although I intended to be on the defensive, I thank you most warmly for that tenderness which enabled you to see my aim and objects throughout a long and necessarily miscellaneous work. And I believe that the way in which you have treated this our *bonâ fide* "endeavour to find a basis for reunion on the principles debated between Archbishop Wake and the Gallican Divines two centuries ago," will, by rekindling hope, give a strong impulse towards that reunion.

Despair is still. If hope is revived in the English mind that Christendom may again be united, rekindled hope will ascend in more fervent prayer to Him who "maketh men to be of one mind in a house," and our prayers will not return unheard for want of love.

Your obedient servant,

E. B. PUSEY.

Christ Church: Nov. 22, 1865.

Second Letter of Dr. Pusey to the "Weekly Register."

SIR,—Will you allow me a few words in explanation, in consequence of Canon Oakeley's remarks on my letter to you, which breathe the kindness of never-forgotten years, but in which, perhaps on that very account, he has read my meaning rather in the light of his own wishes for me ?

1. In regard to the Council of Trent, my statement was, "I have long been convinced that there is nothing in the Council of Trent which *could* not be explained satisfactorily to us, if it were explained authoritatively."

I meant by this, that in regard to some of the declarations of the Council of Trent, which, unexplained, present difficulties to us, some of your own theologians, who have spoken with authority, especially in later times, have stated that certain beliefs are sufficient to satisfy the meaning of the Council on these subjects. If the Church of Rome could formally declare that those beliefs were alone *de fide*, I believe that the great difficulty to reunion on our side would be removed. I could not call this "holding all Roman doctrine;" for this would, in my mind, involve (1) holding the doctrine in the way in which it is commonly and popularly held among you, whether *de fide* or no; (2) holding the doctrine on the authority of Rome, which, not being a member of the Roman Communion, I, of course, do not. Rather, it is holding a faith, which I received (at a time when we never read a Roman book), through writers of our Church, from early tradition, as expounding authoritatively Holy Scripture. On comparing my belief with that expressed by the Council of Trent, I thought that its terms, as explained by some individual doctors, yet of authority among you, did not condemn what I believed, and did not require me to believe what I did not believe. I thought that the Council of Trent so explained for the Church of England, might be a basis of union. If I may sum up briefly, I think that not only on the whole range of doctrine, on the Holy Trinity, and the Incarnation, but also on Original Sin and Justification, and all the doctrines of Grace, there is nothing to be explained; that on the Canon of Scripture, the Holy Eucharist, and the anointing of the sick, there is what has to be mutually explained; that on what I suppose you will account points of lesser magnitude, as those alluded to in our XXII. Article there will be need not only of explanation, but of limitation, what is to be *de fide*.

2. In regard to the Supremacy of the Pope, I

do not know what it involves, nor am I aware
that its limits have been laid down among you.
The Council of Florence, at least according to
the Greek copies, in Archbishop De Marca's
words (De Conc. Sacred et Imp. iii. 8 fin.), declared that "the privileges of the Pope are to be
explained and exercised according to the Canons
and according to the Acts of Œcumenical
Councils, i.e., of the eight Councils, which con-
sisted of the Western and Eastern Church."
But this would leave much to be defined. I
conclude, however, that the Roman Church
cannot hold the Supremacy to be *de fide*, since
it has ever called the Greeks, who reject it,
schismatics, not heretics. In what I wrote I
was thinking of a practical question (as we
English do), what, in the case of a reunion, would
be its effects upon us. You must, anyhow, think
the application of the Supremacy to vary in
different times, since you must believe, that
whatever it be or in whatever it consist, it does
not necessarily involve either (1) the appointment
of the Bishops of a Church in communion with
the See of Rome, by the Pope, nor (2) that the
sanction of the Roman Court must be had, in
order to the *validity* of its Canons, within itself,
nor (3) suppose that *all* appeals should be carried
to Rome. For the two first were unknown to
the Church in St. Augustine's time; and the
third, the African Bishops in Council refused.
And I meant that what we English, as a practical
nation, should feel, would be not an abstract
relation in itself (which might be modified by
Concordats, and would probably, in Henry VIII.'s
time, had that been a time of Concordats), but
such authority as would, by the appointment of

our teachers, soon bring in that whole practical system which is the ground of our remaining as we are.

I have ventured to address this line to you, because I believe full explicitness and openness is essential to all attempts at a better mutual understanding. Difficulties there are, like mountains; but the prayer of faith can remove mountains; and He, whose coming in the Flesh we now rejoice in with the same devotion, can bid every valley be exalted, and every mountain and hill to be made low, and the crooked places to become straight, and the rough places plain, that the glory of God may be revealed, and all flesh see it together.

Your obedient servant,

E. B. PUSEY.

Christ Church, Oxford: Dec. 6, 1865.

THE LIFE OF ROSMINI. 7/6.

THE OLD RELIGION, or How to find Primitive Christianity. 5/-.

THE TEMPORAL SOVEREIGNTY OF THE POPES. 1/-.

THE COMMUNION OF SAINTS. 1/-.

WHO IS THE ANTICHRIST OF PROPHECY? 1/-

ST. ETHELDREDA'S AND OLD LONDON. 1/-.

THE ROMAN AND GOTHIC CHASUBLE. 1/-.
(Illustrated.)

EDITED BY FATHER LOCKHART AND OTHER
FATHERS OF THE ORDER.

Rosmini's Sketch of **MODERN PHILOSOPHIES** and his own System. 1/-.

„ **IDEOLOGY.** 3 vols. 10/- per volume.

„ **PSYCHOLOGY.** 3 vols. 10/- per volume.

ST. THOMAS AND IDEOLOGY. By the Bishop of Casale. 1/-.

IN THE PRESS.

Rosmini's **THEODICY.** 2 vols. 10/- per volume.

College of the Immaculate Conception,

RATCLIFFE, NEAR LEICESTER.

President: The Very Rev. J. HIRST.

RATCLIFFE COLLEGE is situated at the distance of seven miles from Leicester and Loughborough, and within two miles of the Sileby Station, Midland Railway.

The Students are educated for Professional and Mercantile pursuits, the course of Studies comprising what is usually taught in Catholic Colleges: Writing, Arithmetic, Book-keeping, History, Geography, Reading, and Elocution, English Composition, with the Latin, Greek, French, and German Languages, Mathematics and Philosophy.

The College is divided into a Senior and Junior School, with distinct Prefects, Masters, Playgrounds and Dormitories. The age of admission is from 7 to 14.

TERMS:

The pension (to be paid half-yearly in advance), for pupils under 12, is £35 per annum : above that age, £40 per annum.

A Quarter's notice or payment is required previous to the removal of a pupil.

The Midsummer Vacation commences in the middle of July, and ends on the first Monday in September.

For further particulars apply to the President; to the Rev. W. LOCKHART, or the Rev. R. C. BONE, St. Etheldreda's, Ely Place, London, E.C.; to the Rev. J. R. RICHMOND, St. Marie's, Rugby; to the Rev. J. HAYDE, St. Peter's, Cardiff; or to the Rev. M. GARELLI, Upton Co. Cork.